# Love's Redemption

# Deborah McDonald

Deborah McDonald

ISBN: 978-1-954693-77-7

FV6

Printed in the United States

*This is the sixth book in the Over the Bay Series.*

https://deborahmcdonaldauthor.com/

www.IntellectPublishing.com

**Praise for Deborah's previous books....**

*"I liked reading and visually imagining the places she talked about since I'm from the area she talks about. The story is lighthearted and fun."*

-Angela

*"I enjoyed reading this book! Very well written and a great distraction from the stress in life!*

*"*--Amazon Customer

*"A great read. She knows the area and educates those that don't. The romance was real and could be felt by the readers. Can't wait for the next book."*

-Kathleen

Deborah McDonald

# Introduction

I was born in Mobile, Alabama at Providence Hospital. If you took a poll of children born before 1980, I'm sure most would say that's where they were born too. That would be the 'Old Providence', which is no longer. It was on the corner of Springhill Avenue and Catherine Street. It's now an empty lot. WABB was across the street along with a small diner and a building that housed a cleaners. Across the street was a park where my PE class from Little Flower School went for a tennis lesson from James Bivens. From what I remember, Mr. Bivens was a great athlete, or at least that's how I remember him.

I grew up in Oakdale on Bay Avenue until I was seven years old. My father died and our mother moved us to Hannon Avenue in what I still like to call the Loop. I know it may be considered midtown to some, but the Loop always stuck with me. Along with progress by the state, Bay Avenue and all the neighborhoods surrounding it no longer exists either. They've been gone for years. St. Matthew's Church is still there and from what I understand has a steady congregation.

Mobile in the 1970's was not the flourishing downtown area it is today. Maybe others have different memories of those times, but I remember the watering holes, the tired looking streets, the political corruption, and family friends who lost their lives through no fault of their own; robbed when they were trying to work in a grocery store or shot to death.

If you flip a coin, then there are the memories of getting uniforms from Zogby's downtown, shopping at Gayfers, going with our mother to Naman's to get meat and groceries, buying gum from Ladas Pharmacy and waiting outside the old YMCA to catch a Mardi Gras parade with family and friends.

Then as I got older, skating parties, pizza parties at Shakey's and ice cream from Old Dutch became the norm. Then in high school, visits to the mall, the movies and to Godfather's Pizza were popular ways to spend time with friends.

As time marched on, Downtown Mobile had a revitalization. The Exploreum, the Convention Center and the long awaited Maritime Museum all opened. The Crescent Theater became known as a place to watch movies, the bar scene became popular and many restaurants opened downtown. There were many visits to the Peanut Shop. I loved the window displays that Miss Deborah created for every season. There's now Mardi Gras Park that boasts a tree decorated for Christmas and Mardi Gras. The Battle House was reborn, the RSA tower rose above the city and an Electronic Moonpie was attached to the top of what I like to call the old bank building. It just fascinates me when the Moonpie descends from the top of the building during Mardi Gras parades and New Year's Eve. I've gone many a time to the top of the old bank building to eat lunch at Dauphins with friends and family.

As you read *Love's Redemption* you will read about Mobile. But, what I include in this book about the city I was born in is just the tip of the iceberg. You'll come across the neighborhood that one of our main characters, Lillette, lives in. It's called the Oakleigh Garden District, or if you're a native, it's the OGD (and you'll learn about that little Irish pub that's been there for years and years). You'll read about the University of South Alabama and the Fairgrounds. So much history in Mobile.

There's so much I didn't include. What I did include, though, is the man who is the other main character in the book. He's got his work cut out for him. In book five, he was self-serving and Lillette wanted nothing to do with him. He has to redeem himself, which may be hard for many to do. But when something is worth fighting for, maybe it's not so hard after all. Calvin is a police chief, who is good at what he does for a living. Now, he has to be a better man to win the hand of Lillette. I hope you enjoy reading *Love's Redemption.*

Thank you for continuing to read the *Over the Bay Series* and thank you to those who let me know how much you enjoy the books.

Deborah McDonald

# Love's Redemption

Deborah McDonald

# Chapter 1

C alvin Wynfrey, the Police Chief for the city, walked up the steps of Lillette Baker's home in Washington Square on a beautiful Saturday morning in February. He looked around and saw for the first time all the work she had done on her property. He spied the Historic Home marker on the house. The plants, bushes and trees surrounding the house really made it a showcase. As he reached the porch, he saw little touches she had brought to her home: a café table and chairs, potted flowers, and a Mardi Gras flag waving in the breeze. He gazed to the right and saw a swing on the floor of the porch and looked up towards the ceiling, "Guess she hasn't gotten around to that," he thought. The Police Chief shook his head and thought what an ass he'd been to everyone. He hadn't noticed what she had brought into his life. His thoughts had been on having a good time with her on New Year's Eve. In the end he hadn't thought about her after their time together. He regretted his selfishness and his attitude.

One thing he had been able to fix was his relationship with his sister-in-law and her mother. They'd talked a lot over the last three weeks. Even the detective was helping him figure some things out. He was grateful that he was going to be a part of his niece's or nephew's life. He just wondered if it was too late to be a part of the person's life that lived in this house. He'd recovered from his injuries when he had been hit by a car in Daphne earlier in the month. He wasn't sure, but he thought she had come to see him in the hospital. He could have imagined it, but it seemed so real.

Calvin knocked on the glass pane on the door and waited for her to answer. He saw her look through the curtain and then open the door. Lillette stood in the doorway, dressed in workout clothes, her chestnut hair up in a ponytail and her arms crossed with an inscrutable look on her face. He had forgotten how beautiful she was. At this moment, hazel-colored eyes looked at him in disbelief, "Chief, are you lost? I can't think of why you'd be standing at my door." Her eyes clouded with anger and disappointment, "Oh, I can think of one thing you might have on your mind, but I don't remember extending an invitation for you to stay the night. Apparently, that was null and void after New Year's. So, if you'll excuse me."

He held up a hand and stepped forward, "I want to apologize to you. I said some things I shouldn't have last time I saw you and I'm deeply sorry. Thinking of others hasn't been my strong suit lately. I'd like to make it up to you."

She wasn't about to make it easy on him. She was glad that he was out of the hospital. But if Lillette was honest, she had only herself to blame for what he thought of her. She wanted to be with him, but wanted a relationship, not a night here or there. She wasn't used to drinking and had too much that night. Even though she tried not to make excuses, she should have had more self-control. Her eyes moistened, "I just don't know what to say to you. It's my fault what you think of me. I know that. You think I'm just a good-time girl, but I'm more than that, much more. I'm smart and I work hard to make this community and this city shine. I guess I wasn't too smart when it came to you."

He moved to hug her and she backed away. He held up his hands, "Okay, I won't touch you, but please listen to what I want to say. You are more than just a party girl. I am so sorry I ever said that. If my brother Sidney was alive, he'd be so disappointed in me." He shook his head and wiped his eyes, "My brother and I were going to conquer the world. We had it going on there for a while. He and Georgia had a good life over the bay helping young adults and building their own careers. I was over here making my way up the law enforcement ladder in order to protect this city." He smiled, "Lillette, you're not the only one who wants this city to shine. I'm proud of what the citizens of this community have built. Downtown has been in the midst of a revitalization for a long time and it's only getting better. But it's not just about Downtown. It's about the whole city. It's an exciting time and I'm so glad to be a part of it." He smiled at her, "I'd like to share that with you. I think we'd make a good team."

She gazed at him and tempered her response. She leaned over and picked up a basketball from the container inside the door, shouldered her bag and held her keys in her hand. He backed up as she locked the door. She turned to him, "Chief, right now I have a date to play basketball with a group of kids at the community center." Her eyes found his, "Regardless of my behavior at New Year's, it's my nature to weigh my options and to decide if something will be right for me. So, if you'll excuse me." He watched her get into her car and put on her seatbelt. She looked up at him once more then her gaze moved as she started her car and drove away. He touched the banister at the top step, then studied the swing on the porch. He smiled and walked to his car to run an errand. Calvin was going to make sure he did everything in his power to get back in her good graces. She was worth it. They were worth it.

Later that afternoon, Lillette pulled into her driveway, turned the motor off and took a deep breath. Not only had she spent time at the community center, but she also went to her mother's to help with her garden. She pulled down the visor and looked at her face in the tiny mirror. A hot and sweaty woman looked back at her. "Ugh," she said as she put the visor back up. She grabbed her water bottle and her bag, then closed the door. She took a minute to appreciate the big oak trees, her bushes and her monkey grass bordering her sidewalk. She smiled and headed up the stairs. Turning her key in the door, she froze as she looked to the right side of her porch. Dropping her bag, she walked over and gazed at the swing hanging from the ceiling.

Glancing at the big red bow tied to the swing, she spied a card taped to the side of the bow. Plucking the card from the tape, she noticed the name, "Angel" scrawled on the front of the envelope. She walked back down her steps and looked around. Nothing unusual stood out on the street, so she jogged back up her steps and made it over to the swing. She placed her hand on the seat and pressed down. She reached her hand up and pulled on the chain. "So far, so good," she thought. Lillette sat down gingerly, but then put all her weight on the seat. She pushed off gently. Laughing nervously, she pushed a little bit more. She closed her eyes and tilted her head back until it was resting on the back of the swing. She felt the breeze on her face and the wind in her hair. She was in heaven and enjoyed the back and forth movement until she remembered the card in her hand. Pulling open the envelope and removing the card inside, she read aloud, "Beautiful Lillette—At first I thought I was being visited by an angel in the hospital who looked like you. That angel was a vision of hope who gave me the strength to heal and face life again. I would like you to be a part of that life. But I'll take your friendship. Only an angel would be willing to be so kind to me after what I put you through. I hope swinging on your porch brings you the same kind of joy that you give to this city and to me. All the best…Calvin."

She sighed. She wanted to leave those memories of New Year's right where they belonged, but her mind had other ideas. She remembered all they shared. They had been so in tune with each other, anticipating one another's needs into the wee hours. What he didn't know is that regardless of how she had been with him that night and the next morning, she had only been with one other man in her life. She'd been so naïve. She thought loving the man she had dated for two years had meant he'd want to share her life, but he only wanted to share her bed. Much like Calvin, she thought. But maybe she was wrong about him. She rested her hand on the chain of the swing. Life was too short to let regrets overpower the good things in life. She got up and picked up her bag, rooting around for her phone. She dialed the number she thought she'd never use again. He picked up right away.

Dusk had fallen on the historic home in the heart of Washington Square. As Calvin made his way up the steps, he looked to the right and there she was, ensconced on the swing, waiting for him. The candles she had lit cast a cozy glow on the cafe table and rested beside a covered tray of fruit and cheese next to a bottle of wine. She was beautiful in a long sleeve flowing dress, a sweater draped around her. Her hair was tamed into a braid that fell across her shoulder. He thought she looked lovely. He handed over the flowerpot and was pleased with her response, "Snapdragons! Oh, how beautiful. Thank you, Calvin." She got up from the swing and placed the container on her porch. She poured wine in the two glasses she set out earlier and handed him one. She asked, "Do you think the swing will hold us both?"

His gaze landed on her face and he grinned, "Yes ma'am. A master of home repair and renovation put that swing up. It will stay there for life." He gestured for her to sit and he joined her. They both got comfortable, leaned back on the swing, looked at each other and smiled. He spoke up, "So far, so good."

She laughed, "Yes, I said the very same thing earlier when I tried it out." She sipped her wine and said, "Thank you. I've been meaning to raise it up there for some time, but just kept putting it off. There were always more important things to tackle." They swung in companionable silence until she spoke again, "I need to ask you something."

"Go ahead," he replied.

"Are you in love with your sister-in-law?" she asked.

He shook his head, "No, I'm not."

"Huh. I thought you were looking to marry her and help raise her baby."

He shook his head again and gazed at her, "Well, you sure keep your ear to the ground, don't you?"

She shrugged, "I pay attention." She waited for his response.

He sighed, "I thought that's what my brother would have wanted me to do and for a while it's what I thought I wanted too. I don't know why I thought that. Kind of seems tawdry now that I think about what I put her and her mom through. Georgia didn't feel that way about me. She loved my brother and when he died, she didn't transfer that love to me. I thought she might look at me as someone to lean on since I was family. I guess I thought I loved her. I think I just was looking for any ties to my brother." He looked away, "I miss him very much. He was good to me." He felt a hand land on his and he squeezed it. He looked at Lillette sitting next to him and he continued, "I'm not in love with her. I do love her and the little one, though, because they're my family. Of course, she's getting married to Drew Myers, the detective who works in the precinct in Daphne."

She nodded her head, "How do you feel about that?"

"He's a good cop and I think they're great together." He glanced at her, "But don't tell him I said that. I wouldn't want to inflate his ego." He grinned, "I wish he did have a big ego because then it would be easier not to like him. We're still getting used to each other. We've had our share of conflicts, but I think we've pretty much resolved much of those. We both want what's best for Georgia and the baby." He glanced at her, "Does that answer your question?"

She nodded, "You know, tomorrow's Sunday. I missed the afternoon session of the Beethoven and Blue Jeans concert today. There's another one lined up for tomorrow afternoon. I usually try to go every year." She glanced at him.

"Want some company?" he asked, waiting for her answer.

"Maybe I'll ask Gavin, my brother's best friend. See if he's free to go with me. He likes concerts and enjoys going places with me. He and I have gone to movies, museums, and restaurants. We talk about all sorts of things and he's very respectful to me. He's always kind and always thinks of others." Her mouth curved a bit, "And, I've never spent the night with him. He seems to like me anyway."

He gave a short laugh and rubbed his head, "I guess I deserved that."

She shrugged, "So, you busy tomorrow?"

He picked up her hand slowly. Since she didn't pull it away, he kissed her hand and replied, "Yes, I'm busy going to a concert with the beautiful woman sitting next to me."

"That's good to know." She glanced at his dress shirt, pressed pants, and tie. "By the way, you look very nice tonight."

He remarked, "Well, it is a special occasion."

"Oh, yeah?" she asked.

"Oh, yeah. I get to sit on the swing that I'm so grateful hasn't fallen with the woman I'm glad is giving me a second chance."

"Me too." She reveled in the company and in the peaceful movement of the swing, "Want to stay for dinner? I have a roast in the crockpot that should be done along with a salad and some potatoes. We can eat out here on the porch. It's a nice night. What do you say?"

He kissed her hand again and said, "I would love to. What can I do to help?"

She gazed at him and her mouth curved as she replied, "Follow me."

With plates filled, he held the door for her as she brought her dinner outside with napkins and silverware. They sat their plates down and she was about to sit in the chair when he asked her to wait. He stepped to her chair and held it out for her. She took a breath and said, "Thank you, Calvin."

His eyes focused on her face, "You're welcome."

They sat and ate dinner on the front porch with the candlelight flickering and the radio she had plugged in playing soft music. After dinner, he helped her put the dishes in the dishwasher and they came back out to the porch and sat in the swing once more. He put his arm around her and she laid her head on his shoulder. He spoke up, "I want to ask you something. That first night when I was in the hospital, I opened my eyes and thought you were there. I was kind of out of it and thought it must have been my imagination. I didn't think you wanted anything to do with me." When she didn't say anything, he continued, "I clung to the fact that maybe you did come to see me and maybe you still liked me. It gave me hope that I could make things right with you." She raised her head and looked at him. She leaned over and gently touched his lips. He cupped her cheek and let her take the lead. It was a sweet kiss. One he probably didn't deserve. He kissed her on the forehead and she laid her head back on his shoulder.

When their night ended, she blew out the candles. He walked her to the door and she turned to him, "Thank you again for putting my swing up. I had a nice night." She leaned over and kissed his cheek, "Goodnight, Calvin. I'll see you tomorrow."

He stepped back, "Goodnight." He put his hands in his pockets and waited for her door to close. When he heard the locks engage on the other side, he turned and walked to his car, smiling all the way.

The next afternoon, Calvin climbed the steps he had gone up the night before and looked at the swing on the porch, "Still up there. Damn, I'm good." Chuckling, he gently tapped his knuckles on the door. When it opened, he took a breath. Her chestnut colored hair was down in all its glory and she was a knockout in a white button down, sweater and jeans. He spoke up, "If you don't mind me saying so, you've got it going on. You look amazing."

She smiled, "Hi, Calvin." She gave him a look and replied, "Well, apparently I'm not the only one who's got it going on. You look very handsome." He looked down at his navy blue shirt and jeans topped with his city insignia jacket.

"Well, I appreciate that." He held out his arm, "Ready to go?" She locked her door and took his arm. He escorted her to his car, a black 1966 Mustang convertible.

"Calvin, does this belong to you? I thought you drove a Honda."

He opened her door, "This baby here usually stays in my garage. Every so often I've had people that weren't too happy with me and I've discovered flat tires, doors that have been keyed, and scrapes on my car. When you're in my position, sometimes arrests and warrants aren't taken too kindly, so I usually drive the Honda, which I've had forever or my Take-Home vehicle. I only bring Carla out on special occasions."

She glanced at him, "Oh my God. You named your car? You're one of those guys?" She shook her head.

"Alright, no judgement here now. I'm taking you out in a fine car today. You should thank me for bringing her around to get you. Now, we can always take her back home and pick up the Honda." He waited for her response as he was smiling inside at the changing expressions on her face.

She glanced at him and asked, "Special occasions, huh?" He nodded. He had his hand on the door waiting for her to get in when she put her hand on his. She then looked at him and said, "Thank you, Calvin."

A smile reached his eyes, "You're welcome." As she settled in the seat, he closed her door. As he rounded the car, he looked to heaven, "Thank you little brother. She's a special lady and I need all the help I can get." He got into the car, winked at his companion, and revved the motor.

She laughed and exclaimed, "Are you serious? Oh my God!" She looked around as she put on her seatbelt, "You know this is the Oakleigh Garden District." She waved her fingers in front of his face, "You know, the OGD?" She rolled her eyes at him and continued, "Remember, I have to live here. Revving the motor. Good Lord." She looked at him, grinned and settled back for the ride in a classic. He smiled at her and then in an about face, drove slowly down the street, which made her laugh even more.

# Chapter 2

Two weeks flew by with Calvin in a flurry of dinners, going to events in the city or just sitting on the swing on her front porch. Lillette was being courted for the first time in her life and she was having a ball. As she got out of her car, she looked at the front of the business. She saw a cut-out of a worm wearing glasses coming out of an apple. *The Bookworm* was the name of Georgia Wynfrey's bookstore. "Clever. Very clever," she thought. She learned that Calvin's birthday was coming up and knew just whom to ask for help. As she entered the store, she glanced around and was charmed. She spied the glassed-in room where parents and kids were working on puzzles or reading together. She saw all the books shelved fastidiously and the cute line of gifts near the register.

"Welcome to The Bookworm. May I help you?"

Lillette looked up and said the first thing that came to her mind, "Wow, you look just like Halle Barry."

The woman in front of her smiled, 'Yeh, I get that a lot." She pressed her hand to her back and stretched.

"You okay? Do you need to sit down?"

"Oh, no. I'm sorry. Just the little one wanting attention. I'm all good. Is this your first time here?" asked Georgia.

"Yes. Actually, I should introduce myself. I'm Lillette Baker."

Before she could say anymore, the bookstore owner spoke up, "Lillette. You're dating Calvin, my brother-in-law." She took a breath, "May I just say you are beautiful. I envy all that hair you have." She touched her pixie cut, "This just seems to work for me." She took a breath and said, "It's very nice to meet you. If I must say, he is quite glad you gave him another chance."

She took a breath, "Oh, so he's talked to you about me?"

Georgia put a hand on her arm, "He came to see me and wanted to talk. He said he made a mistake about something he said to you." She noticed the young woman's eyes shift to hers and said, "He didn't tell me what he said or go into it, but I could tell it bothered him greatly. You know, Calvin and I have had a rough time with our share of ups and downs, mostly due to mistakes he made, but we're finally on the same page. He likes you very much. He said you're one in a million and he was so sorry that he hurt you by what he said. You might say he has turned things around for himself and he's trying to be a better person and lead a happier life. Sounds like he wants you to be a part of that life."

Lillette nodded, "Yes, you might say he's courting me." She saw the surprise in the bookstore owner's face and smiled at her. "He's been wooing me by sitting on the swing he put up for me on my porch. He'll come over some evenings and we'll swing and talk. He brought me a pot of snapdragons and even helped me weed my garden."

Georgia raised an eyebrow, "My, he has been busy." She touched the young woman's arm, "Good for you. I'm glad."

Lillette took a breath and responded, "Yes, it doesn't sound like he said anything to you about this part, but we kind of dove into our relationship too quickly, I guess you could say. We had to step back and start over with each other." She raised her eyes to meet Georgia's, "I'm glad we did. I really like him. In fact, I've wanted to go out with him for a long time but was too nervous to do anything about it." She took another breath, "So, when he and I were at the New Year's Eve gala, I guess you could say things escalated too fast. It was just too soon for us to appreciate what we could have with each other in the long run. I think we know that now."

"I'm happy for you. Now, is there anything I can help you with today in the store? We have books on gardening, romances, mysteries, magazines and a coffee bar."

She smiled at the bookstore owner, "Actually, his birthday is coming up and I wanted to get him something. That's why I came here. I knew you owned the shop and wanted to ask for ideas or suggestions."

"You're right. He's turning 35. He's two years older than my Sid." Lillette watched her touch her stomach and smile. "Let's see, he likes baseball and he loves that city he watches over every day. Have you thought about tickets to a game or taking him to one of the restaurants downtown?"

"Yes, but I think I want something else for him. When he took me for a ride in his Mustang, I thought about a book on classic cars or tickets to the Mustang Museum or membership. I had no clue that there's a Mustang Museum of America in Alabama."

"Wait," said the bookstore owner, "He took Carla out of his garage and took you for a ride? Wow, this is serious. I knew he really liked you, but you do understand that he only takes that car out for…."

Lillette interrupted, "Yes, for special occasions." She smiled at Georgia and then had to laugh, "He even revved the motor in my neighborhood."

Georgia looked at her like she had two heads, "Calvin Wynfrey was showing off for you. Oh my, he really wants to make a good impression if he brought Carla out." Her eyes moistened, "I'm so glad for you. You're very special if he's taking the time to do all this for you."

Lillette began to say something when a handsome man walked up to Georgia with two take-out bags and kissed her on the mouth. He said, "Hey, Bookworm. They were out of the bacon burger, so I got you a plain salad and orange slices." He snickered, then gently touched her stomach, and smiled.

"Ha ha. You're hilarious." She looked at the young woman in front of her, "Lillette, this is my Drew. He's a detective here in the city and about to be my husband and father to this little one I'm carrying. Drew, this is Lillette Baker."

"Calvin's Lillette? Nice to meet you. If I may say so, he's a lucky man."

"Well, nice to meet you too. It's like Hollywood royalty in here. You do realize you look like that actor from the movie *Knives Out*?" She watched his fiancé nod her head.

He sighed, "I just don't see it. Why does everyone keep telling me that?"

"Because it's true!" the two women exclaimed in unison.

"Well, I'll just go set up lunch in your office." He bent to kiss her on the head, "I will see you in there shortly. Lillette, it's nice to meet you. Oh, one more thing. Calvin's a good cop and he's coming along in being a friend. Just don't tell him I said that. The man has a huge ego." He winked at her and smiled as he walked to Georgia's office.

Lillette just laughed and shook her head, "Well, I appreciate anything you can help me with."

Georgia nodded, "I do have some books on classic cars. How about a magazine subscription? You'd have to snoop if you go to his house to see what magazines are out on his coffee table. When Sid and I would visit, he used to keep some car magazines lying around in his living room. I just don't remember which ones." She took a breath, "I do like your idea of the Mustang Museum tour and membership. I've never heard him talk about that and he and my Sid used to talk about cars and baseball all the time. That would be a different gift. Also, tickets to a baseball game would be good. He likes the JAGS since he went to school there. What do you think?"

"I think I'm glad I got to meet you and Drew and I'm glad I came over here today. Thank you so much. Now, if you'll point me in the direction of those car books, I'll let you go have lunch with your detective."

Georgia said, "Come on, I'll show you. It will just take a minute. I'm so glad to meet you too. We have a lot to talk about. Someday, when you have more time, let me know and we'll go to lunch across the street. They have these amazing fish tacos." Lillette smiled and followed the bookstore owner down the aisle.

It was another hectic week for the Planning Events Coordinator for the city, but Lillette finally had everything ready to celebrate Calvin's birthday. They had been seeing each other for a few weeks now and she had the whole evening planned. It was Friday night and she was taking him to an elegant downtown restaurant 34 floors up with panoramic views of the city and the bay. The Creole food there was excellent. She loved seeing him dressed in his suits. He was one fine looking man. She grinned because she was so excited to be going out with him. She put her hand on her heart. Everything was still so new. If she was honest with herself, she had been smitten with him for a long time. She looked at the time and realized she needed to leave if she was going to be ready to be picked up at 7:00. She got on the elevator and before the doors closed, she was soon joined by Noah Webster, the Executive Director of Public Safety. He turned to her, "Well, hello Lillette. My, aren't you looking very pretty these days. You seem to have a glow about you."

Lillette didn't say anything as she never cared for the man standing in the elevator with her. He was nice looking with sandy brown hair, blue eyes and always dressed in a suit. She couldn't quite put her finger on it, but something about him always seemed off, like he was being condescending to people while keeping a pleasant smile on his face.

He continued, "I understand you and the Chief of Police have been going out. That's an interesting choice for you, him being an older man and all." She felt him staring at her and not in a good way, "You know, I remember asking you out a few times, but you always turned me down and the excuses you gave me were always job related. I guess on New Year's Eve, you finally had an evening off and decided to spend it with the Chief." She wasn't going to give him the satisfaction of an answer, but she fingered her key ring until she gripped the pepper spray in her hand. He took a step towards her and said, "Seems like you two hit it off, especially since I saw you leave together." As she was about to raise her hand, the elevator opened. She moved forward to her car in the parking lot. He followed her and she took a breath, but then realized his car was parked next to hers. He looked at her one more time, "Lillette, if you do get tired of being with Calvin, you just let me know. We'd have a good time, you and me. I'd make sure of it. Good night now."

She quickly got in her car and locked the doors. She took a deep breath and started her car, "Creep." Lillette had many contacts in this city, including the mayor. She wasn't about to put up with Noah's obvious harassing remarks. She wouldn't say anything to Calvin yet, since it was their special night. But, if she needed to, she would later. Right now, she had a new dress to get into when she got home. She thought of Calvin and smiled.

# Chapter 3

A t 7:00 on the dot, Calvin was walking to her door. It was about to be Mardi Gras time in the city and this was probably going to be the last weekend he had free before their department would be inundated with extra patrols and crowd control. He straightened his tie and held a bouquet of roses in his hand, which was shaking because he was nervous. He looked down at his suit and pocket square and muttered, "Get it together, Calvin. You're not a teenager. Jesus." He smoothed his hand over his head and adjusted his tie. This was their first big evening out for an elegant occasion since they started dating each other. He was 35 today and looking forward to celebrating with her. He took a breath and rang the bell.

Lillette jumped a little when she heard the doorbell, but then a smile blossomed on her face. She turned to look in the full length mirror in her bedroom. She was wearing an elegant knee-length 1950's vintage dress cinched at the waist with a wide belt. Her mom had bought her the dress when she had learned about her big evening with Calvin. Lillette had swept her hair up and was wearing her grandmother's pearls and pearl earrings. She took the sheer silvery wrap off the back of her chair and put it on. She took another deep breath and tried to calm her emotions.

This was a special night for Calvin and she wanted them to have a nice time. If she was honest with herself, she was worried about what would happen after dinner. He seemed to be happy with their relationship. She wasn't ready for anything else. There might be a point in their relationship when they'd have to talk about the next step. Lillette would be firm in her stance in wanting an old-fashioned romance. She turned her head when she heard the bell ring for the second time. She spoke aloud, "Okay, Lillette. Quit worrying and just enjoy tonight." She smoothed her hands down the sides of her dress and walked to the door. When she opened it, she was breathless at his appearance, "Hi Calvin. You look wonderful." She moved forward and kissed his cheek.

He had no words. He finally cleared his throat, "Lillette, you are a vision. My God, you are beautiful!" He returned the kiss on her cheek and held out the roses, "These are for you."

"Calvin, they're gorgeous. Thank you." She gestured, "Come in and let me put these in a vase."

He followed her to the kitchen where he watched her fill a crystal vase with water before placing the bouquet in the vase. He heard her say, "I think I'll put them on the dining room table." He was right behind her as she placed the roses on the table. When she straightened, she turned and he was very close to her.

"Lillette, I know we are taking our time with our relationship, but I really would love to kiss you. You are one elegant lady and I'm so proud to be with you. You are breathtaking."

She put her hands in his, "Calvin, you look very dapper in your suit." She smiled, "Do people even use that word anymore?"

He pulled her hand up and kissed it, "We do." He leaned forward and his lips touched hers tentatively. He moved back a step and looked into her eyes, "Lillette, you have become very important to me. I hope you feel the same way."

She gazed at him, "Yes, I do. I like what we have." She looked at him again, "May I say once more how great you look in your suit."

He laughed softly, "Thank you. I can only say that you are class defined." He kissed her hand once more, "I'm afraid if we don't go now, I'd be tempted to stay here and kiss you all night."

She placed her hand on his cheek and gave him a sweet smile, "I'm ready." He walked her out the door and waited while she locked up. As she turned she smiled again, "Ah, Carla is joining us tonight." She observed his smile as he helped her into the car. She also saw him gaze at her legs. She looked at him in reproach, but her eyes were twinkling.

He grinned, "Okay, you caught me. What do you want from me?" He thought she was sexy as hell, but he wasn't going to say that out loud, since he really wanted to make a good impression on her. "You are all wrapped up in grace and sophistication. I can't help what you do to me." He closed her door and came around to get settled in the seat next to hers.

She gazed at him demurely as a small smile showed on her face, "How 'bout you keep your eyes on the road?"

He looked back at her, winked and revved the mustang's engine before cruising down the street, both of them sharing a laugh as they made their way to the restaurant.

All too soon, Carla was bringing them home. Calvin came to her door and helped her out of the car. He walked her to the house and stood behind her as she unlocked her door. Once inside and the door was closed, he gathered her in his arms and said, "Thank you." He kissed her gently on the mouth as she held on to him. He continued, "I enjoyed the hell out of my birthday. The food was terrific, the view outstanding and the company couldn't have been any better. I loved all the gifts you gave me too." He kissed her on the nose then shook his head and grinned, "How you got Lisa Mills to sing Happy Birthday to me I'll never know."

Lillette kissed him on the cheek, "I happened to be at the Fairgrounds early last summer when she was singing in the concert series. I remember seeing you grin and even sing along with some of her songs on the sidelines. You couldn't take your eyes off her. Then when the mayor introduced you to her, I thought you were going to kneel at her feet, you look so dazzled when she talked to you."

"How do you remember things like that?" he asked.

"I pay attention," she replied. She took a deep breath, "That's the moment when I realized I wouldn't mind going out with you. I liked your smile. Right after that concert, your brother died. I'm so sorry too, because after that you were so unhappy and I missed your smile." He put his hand on her cheek and lowered his head for a kiss. She didn't disappoint him as her eyes moistened and she kissed him back. He wiped the few tears

32

that fell from her eyes. She took a few seconds and then composed herself, "You've forgotten my job as a Planning Events Coordinator puts me in touch with many singers. I had a contact who set it up. I was fortunate to find out she was in town and was happy to do it. You see, she remembered you and thought it was sweet that I would do something like this for you."

He hugged her as she held onto him, "Well, I would like to thank you again for such a nice night."

"Well, the night's not over yet." She gestured to the dining room table, "You sit down and I'll be right back." She went to the kitchen. He sat down as he heard her rummaging in the drawers and heard her open and shut the fridge. She then put two big candles on the table and lit them and then she turned off the light. He smiled as she doubled back into the kitchen and brought out a small bowl with a candle burning on top of what was in the bowl. She stood in front of him and said, "Okay, make a wish and blow out your birthday candle." He did as she asked. She set the candle on the birthday napkin she put on the table and continued talking, "Now, close your eyes." He closed his eyes. When she made sure he was cooperating, she took a spoon and dipped it into the cup, "I want you to keep your eyes closed and open your mouth."

He gave her a look and sighed, "I'm a cop and I always need to know what's going on around me. Because it's you, I'll do it. But only because this must be a special moment." He closed his eyes.

"I got it. Now, don't peek and open your mouth." As he did what she asked, she put the spoon in his mouth and he tasted what was on the spoon. She spoke up, "Sometimes things taste better with your eyes closed."

His eyes popped open, "Is that what I think that is?" She nodded her head and smiled as he uttered, "Oh my God! That's Chocolate Sin Delight. How did you know?"

"When I talked to Georgia, she told me that it was what you and your brother liked to eat for dessert. She said it was y'all's favorite and that you'd have it for every birthday. She would even make it for you both after she married Sidney."

"You talked to Georgia?" he asked.

"Yes, I went to her store, which by the way is amazing! I introduced myself and asked for some ideas for your birthday. She gave me a list of ingredients and I made it today before you picked me up."

"Did you try it?" he asked.

She shook her head, "Calvin, with the dinner we ate tonight, I'm not allowed to have any dessert. Besides, it's your birthday."

"Lillette Baker, this is your lucky night." He dipped his spoon into the dessert and held it out for her, "Now, it's time for you to close your eyes and taste one of the most luscious desserts ever known to man. Here."

She shook her head, "Calvin Wynfrey, I'll try anything at least once, but I draw the line at eating or drinking after someone, even you. I use my own silverware and my own bowl. I don't share. Never have and my mother didn't either."

"You mean to tell me that you and your mom never shared the same Coke can or ate off the same fork or spoon when it came to sharing birthday cake or dessert?" he asked.

"We just were never like that." She held up a clean spoon, "However, I do have my own spoon and I wouldn't mind trying it."

He held up his hand, "Uh uh. Close your eyes." She did as he asked and before he could dip her spoon in the bowl, she opened one eye. He chuckled, "I promise you it's your spoon." He shook his head and muttered, "Lord, I've had my mouth on yours, kissing you, yet you won't share my spoon. It just boggles the mind." She closed her eyes again and savored the flavor of chocolate pudding and cool whip.

She then took the bowl from him and took her spoon to eat the rest of what was in the bowl. He spoke up, "You better have more in that fridge. You just ate my birthday dessert."

She put her hand over her mouth and swallowed the dessert, then grinned, "Yes, there's more in the fridge." She went to go into the kitchen and his hand captured her arm. She looked at him with a question in her eyes.

"For my birthday, I want you to do something for me."

She asked, "What would that be?"

He pulled her down until she was sitting on his lap and looked at his watch, "I have a couple of hours left of my birthday. I'd like you to sit here for a while with me." He wrapped his arms around her, "I just want to hold you if that's okay with you. I like being close to you and I've had such a good time tonight. I'd just like it to last a little bit longer before I have to go home." She leaned back into his arms and enjoyed cuddling with him.

"If I don't watch it, I'll fall asleep right here in your arms. You feel so good and you make me feel so safe," she murmured.

He put his head on top of hers and she could feel when a smiled bloomed on his face, "Someday I wouldn't mind waking up with you in my arms. But for tonight, I like being here with you just like this. Think you can get your Alexa to play some Ella Fitzgerald or some Billie Holiday for me to round out my birthday?"

She nodded and found Ella Fitzgerald on her Alexa. She put her head back on his chest. His arms tightened and he held her. After about 15 minutes he had to smile. His Lillette, who had more energy than most people, had fallen asleep in his arms. He held her and thought it was the best birthday present he had ever received in his life.

# Chapter 4

Lillette woke up on Saturday morning, rolled over and looked at her phone on her bedside table. She thought she heard ringing. It was only 7:00 and she knew she hadn't set an alarm. She told her mother yesterday morning that since it was going to be a big night for Calvin's birthday, that she wouldn't be joining her for breakfast. They usually tried to go to different restaurants on Saturday mornings to talk about the week, but she'd make it up to her. She listened again. Sure enough, someone was at her door, ringing her bell. She grabbed a sweatshirt and threw it on over her tank she wore with her leggings. As she got to the door, she looked out of the curtain and opened the door. Blinking at the bright sun, she asked, "Calvin? Do you know what time it is?"

He came in and kissed her on the cheek, "Yes, it's time for our run. Don't you remember?" She looked at him and it registered that he had on running shorts and a Torch-Run t-shirt.

She held her forehead and shook her head, "I fell asleep and don't remember much after that."

"Well, Sunshine, you fell asleep in my arms at your dining room table. I woke you up and we talked about taking a run this morning. You got my dessert out of your fridge last night and gave the rest of it to me to take home. Then when you walked me to the door, you said you wouldn't mind getting in some exercise this morning. I told you I'd meet you here and take you out to South to run. Lots of room out there at the university and it's a great place to walk or get in a run."

"First of all, let me apologize for falling asleep on you during your birthday. I'm very embarrassed about that."

"Well, hey, don't worry about that. I mean, you didn't drool or snore, so that was a win for me." He winked at her and grinned.

"Ha ha ha." She sighed, "Okay, quick shower to wake up and I'll be good to go. There's coffee in the kitchen. I use a timer so it should be ready. I have juice, some fruit and water in the fridge. Help yourself." She stared at him, "Are you sure I agreed to this?" He nodded and she walked out of the room.

He couldn't help but grin. She was adorable when she was all soft and warm from her bed. He had to take a deep breath and make himself not follow her when that's all he wanted to do. But he wasn't about to make that mistake, so he walked into the kitchen and grabbed a mug for coffee. He took it out to her sunroom and made himself at home in one of her rocking chairs and waited.

They conquered six miles together and walked another two miles to cool down. He treated her to a protein shake at the nearest nutrition place and then took her home. He left her at her door with a quick kiss and a promise to pick her up later that afternoon for supper and a sunset.

Since she was already in workout clothes, she weeded her garden and cut the grass. Calvin had offered to help her with her

38

yard anytime she wanted, but she liked the feeling of doing it herself and it helped her stay fit. She sat on the back steps sipping a glass of ice water and looking at the beauty of her backyard. She really did love living here. Sighing and looking at her lawnmower and gardening tools, she realized they weren't going to move themselves. Putting everything up in her shed took a while as she began to organize the chaos of some boxes she had thrown in there and placing tools where they needed to go so it wouldn't be so cluttered. Lillette glanced at her watch, "Oh, shoot! Calvin will be here any minute and I need a quick shower." She had worked through lunch and hadn't realized the time. She walked in her back door and turned to close it. Before she could do that, an arm snaked around her neck and held her there. She tried to pry loose and began to kick her back leg out, and the man that held her blocked her kick. She tried to remember her defense moves training and couldn't get out of his hold.

"Don't move, keep your mouth shut and I won't hurt you. I want cash and your car keys and I want them now." She tried to break loose and he twisted her arm up behind her and she yelled at the pain that shot up her arm. "Goddammit, didn't I tell you to be quiet? You're in for it now, bitch." She tried breaking away and as she turned she got a hand free and hit him square in the nose. He charged her and she screamed before the breath was knocked out of her as they sailed through the open back door. Landing on the grass, she tried scooting away as fast as she could, but the man grabbed her by the ankle. She looked back and saw he had a knife in his hand. She kicked out as he gripped her ankle tight and started to twist it. She felt his grip loosen, realized she was free and started to run. Lillette heard a shout and a grunt behind her. She looked over her shoulder and then stopped.

Calvin had the man face down in the grass, a knee on his back, the knife gone. Two officers rounded into the backyard, their weapons drawn. One of the officers handed over his cuffs which Calvin quickly used on the perpetrator. He looked down on the ground and saw the weapon. He pulled out a handkerchief and covered the knife with it and handed it over to one of the officers, "Okay, he's ready. Take him in." It took all of the Chief's patience and training not to want to have five minutes alone with the man who dared to hurt Lillette. He watched the officers, "EMT's ETA?"

"Yes, Chief, they'll be here inside of two minutes," answered one of the officers. The Chief of Police nodded.

The man was now being led away by the two officers to their car. He spoke up, "Hey lady! Next time you and me. All night long! Remember, I know where you live." Calvin turned and looked at the man.

He took a step forward and then felt a hand reach for his and he smelled the flowery scent she always wore. "Stay with me Calvin. Please. He's not worth the career you built. He doesn't know us and how much of a team we are. I need you. Please."

He turned his head and noticed the blood dripping down her arm, "Lillette!" He scooped her up at the same time he saw the EMT's coming through to the backyard, "Hey, I'm bringing her to you. Her arm's bleeding and we need to check out the ankle." Then he whispered to her, "Hold on. I've got you and I'm going to make sure you're taken care of."

"Calvin, I'm okay. I just cut my arm on the door when he charged me. I just need some ointment and a big bandage," she said. His blood turned cold and he held her tighter as he carried her to the ambulance. He sat her down and the EMT's checked her out.

Charlie was the name of the first EMT who helped her with her arm, "Ma'am, looks like you have a small piece of wood embedded here." He took some tweezers and pulled it out. He cleaned the wound and put on a bandage. He looked at her ankle and her head to make sure there were no more fragments or bumps anywhere. After the EMT's examined her, Charlie turned to Calvin, "Chief, all clear. We can take her in, but everything looks superficial."

The Chief of Police gazed at her, "What do you think? Headache? Nausea? Anything else we need to have looked over?"

She shook her head and the second EMT whose name was Reese, spoke up, "Ibuprofen or Tylenol will work if needed. Otherwise, I'd take it easy for a couple of days. If anything hurts or you begin to feel worse, then I would suggest you see your doctor for a follow up."

The Chief patted his back and said, "Thanks men. Appreciate the quickness and the efficiency." He picked up Lillette and moved down the sidewalk until he sat her down in the swing on the front porch. He gathered her gingerly in his arms, "I'm going to secure that back door, give you something now to head off any aches and pains, and let you rest. Then, I'm staying. Any problem with any of that?"

She gazed at him, every inch the hard line cop. She could see why he was the Chief. His orders were not to be questioned,

"No sir, Chief." He glanced at her with an inscrutable look as she softened and said, "Calvin, I'm not being a smartass. I would like you to stay."

"I'm talking overnight too. I'm staying the night in the guest room. Understand?" he asked.

She nodded her head, "Can you take me inside now? I'm about to cry, but I don't want to do it on the front porch. We'll have to go around back since the front door is locked." She took a breath, "I want a shower before I get in my bed and I need to call my mom, too. I don't want her hearing about this from anyone else."

He came to her and touched her face, "We'll do all of that now. We are going to do everything possible to make sure this doesn't happen again. I want you protected." He helped her down the steps. As they reached the driveway, her closest neighbors were there making sure she was alright as they had seen the police cars and ambulance. She assured them she was and told them the police had taken care of everything. Calvin then took over, telling her neighbors he needed to get her inside. They told her they were glad she was alright and would check on her later. As they walked away, she heard them talk about their neighborhood watch and safety patrol for the neighborhood. As he saw she was favoring her ankle, he had her lean on him. He helped her straight through the back door into her sunroom and had her sit in one of her rocking chairs.

He got her a bottle of water, two Advil and her phone. He stood by her looking out the window as he heard her replay the events of the afternoon for her mother, his mouth tightening, doing his best to control his anger. She lived in a pretty safe neighborhood, but every so often there'd be a break-in or items stolen from cars that were left unlocked. He hadn't had an assault in this neighborhood since he'd been named Chief. He folded his arms and thought about the citywide meetings he needed to continue about neighborhood watches and increased patrols across the city. He would work on that immediately. He wanted the citizens safe in this city. Crime never took a holiday, but his department worked hard to educate the people in the communities to be smart, to be aware and not to hesitate to call the police. Calvin turned as he realized she had finished her phone call. She was moving slowly and he helped her out of her chair.

Walking with her to her bedroom, he waited while she got fresh clothes and helped her to the bathroom door, "I'm right here if you need me." She touched his arm and nodded. Once she finished in the bathroom, she was walking cautiously, so he picked her up.

"Calvin, I can make it to the bed. I'm just drained and need some sleep."

"I know you can, but just let me do this, okay?" She saw the anger on his face earlier when she was talking to her mom, but now moisture filled his eyes.

She put her hand on his cheek, "Oh, Calvin, baby, I'm okay. I just need to rest. Knowing you will be here with me tonight is going to help me relax. I'm so glad you're staying here."

Reaching the bed, he flipped down the comforter and helped her lie down. Once she was settled, he pulled the cover over her and bent down to kiss her. His control finally broke as he knelt on the floor next to her bed and laid his head on her stomach, "Lillette, I don't know what I would have done if you'd been seriously hurt or worse." His eyes found hers, "You do understand how close I came to throwing out the rule book and taking on that asshole, don't you?"

She nodded as she tried to soothe him by running her hand over his head, "You're a good man, Calvin, and a great Police Chief. The people that want to ruin this city and hurt others aren't worth one-tenth of the integrity you have and the job that you do every day. Thank you for saving me." She yawned, then drifted off to sleep, her hand still on his head. He raised his head and kissed her hand. He watched her for a few minutes, so peaceful in sleep. He left her door slightly ajar in case she needed him, then went out to her sunroom to make those phone calls to secure her home.

Love's Redemption

# Chapter 5

Lillette woke to a wonderful smell. She turned over to look at the clock and realized she had been asleep for three hours. She sat up and put her feet on the floor. She stretched and went to the bathroom to wash her face and brush her teeth. Feeling somewhat normal again, she searched out that tantalizing aroma and landed in the kitchen, only to see Calvin in an apron cooking. He turned towards her and exclaimed, "There's my girl!" He turned the heat down on the skillet and moved over to hug her, "How are you feeling? Any aches or pains?"

She shook her head and just held on to him, loving the feel of his arms around her and the scent of his cologne, now mixed with the scent of the supper he was cooking. She replied, "I'm okay. The nap helped. I didn't realize I slept so long. Thank you for being here." She kissed his cheek and asked, "So, what are we having tonight?"

As he continued to hold her, he replied, "That would be my famous Chicken Cacciatore, seasoned green beans and some excellent crusty bread with butter."

"Did you run to the store?" she asked.

He nodded and kissed her on top of the head, "Your mom came over to check on you, so while she was here, I ran to the store and also picked up my clothes for work tomorrow."

Lillette noticed the cake on the kitchen counter, "You got us a chocolate cake?"

"I baked all afternoon." He looked at her with a gleam in his eye.

"You did not. Sometimes, that poker face of yours doesn't always work."

"Your mom went by *Divine Delights* and picked that up for her daughter and something for me."

She sat down on a stool in the kitchen and asked, "She did what? She got you something?"

"Yes, while she was there, she called me and since I just had a birthday, asked what kind of cake I liked. So, I told her."

Lillette swiveled her head, "Well, where is it?"

"It's in the fridge," he replied as he smiled.

She hopped off the stool and opened the fridge. She turned to him in amazement, "She got you the chocolate drizzle peanut butter filled cake? Do you understand that is like the top of the line dessert at that place? Oh my God, she likes you."

He grinned as he continued to stir their dinner, "I think she does. We talked while you were asleep." He lost his smile, "Of course she scares the hell out of me. She's one tough lady."

"Yeah, she is." She grinned and wrapped her arms around him from behind, "I'm so happy."

He patted one of her hands and looked back at her, "Because you're glad we're together?"

"No, because I get chocolate cake and I'm stealing some of your dessert too." She did a hip bump with him and he leaned down to kiss her. As she hugged his neck they both laughed.

Later that night, full from dinner and dessert, she and Calvin curled up on the couch and watched an old movie. Since she fell asleep half-way through the movie, he kissed her on the head and carried her to her bed. He pulled the covers up over her and she turned over and slept on. He whispered, "You are out like a light." He smoothed her hair back and just looked at her, "You are one beautiful woman. You are smart, wonderful, and kind enough to give me a second chance." He leaned down and kissed her cheek, "Sweet dreams my beautiful Lillette." He walked to the living room and hit the remote to turn off the movie and cleared their coffee cups and dessert plates. Calvin made sure the back door was secure. He checked to make sure all of the windows were locked.

As he finished cleaning up the kitchen, he wanted to remind himself to ask her about an alarm system, training with a weapon or getting a really big dog. She had confided to him that her self-defense training hadn't worked, so he told her he'd take her to some refresher classes. Instead of putting the dishes in the dishwasher, he needed the distraction of washing dishes by hand so he could calm himself every time he thought what could have gone wrong. He was only here this afternoon because he had a date with her. What would have happened if he hadn't have been here? He kept scrubbing dishes and took a deep breath. He needed to give her all the techniques to protect herself so he wouldn't worry. He knew the statistics and the crime data and he didn't want her to be counted as one of those statistics.

As he put the dishes away, he turned off the light, then checked the doors once more to make sure they were locked. He changed into a t-shirt and a pair of gym shorts. Instead of heading to the guest bedroom, he walked to her room. He sat in the rocker in the corner of the room and stretched his legs out on the ottoman. He felt better being in the room with her. He watched her and then before realizing it, fell asleep.

During the night he felt someone near him and opened his eyes. She was standing in front of him with a frightened expression and a blanket in her arms, "Can you hold me?" He moved his arms so she could sit on his lap. She curled her legs up and he pulled the blanket over them both. He gathered her in close and held her. They slept.

The first thing she smelled when she woke up was coffee. She looked around and noticed the time. She was in her bed and alone in the room. She made it to the bathroom slowly, but was able to shower and dress. Lillette put her hair up in a bun and added earrings as well as a little make-up. She pulled on some comfortable shoes due to her sore ankle. She was ready for work. When she landed in the kitchen, he was sitting at the café table drinking a cup of coffee. He got up and pulled her in for a hug. She smiled and said, "I sure do like being greeted by a man all dressed up." She leaned back and he let her go, "You are certainly handsome in that suit, Chief Wynfrey."

"I appreciate that," he hugged her. "Good morning. You're going to tell me why you're dressed for work? I thought the plan was for you to take a day or two just to make sure you're okay."

She reached up and kissed him. When he began to release her from his arms, she pulled him back and just held on to him, "I really appreciated you staying with me last night, although, I don't know how you got any sleep in that rocking chair." She walked over to the counter to pour herself a cup of coffee, "To answer your question, I don't want to stay here today and brood about what happened. I don't want to be afraid to go out to swing by myself, sit on my back steps or go into my shed." The tears then began to roll down her face, "I'm not going to let him take away my home. Do you hear me, Calvin?" He came over to hold her as she continued, "It's not fair. It's just not fair." He held her while she cried. He handed her his handkerchief and she wiped her eyes. As she settled down, she looked at what he gave her and remarked, "I didn't know men carried these anymore. It's nice to see. Thank you. I think I just needed a chance to cry."

He lifted her chin and gave her a soft kiss, "You sure you want to go to work today?" She nodded her head and he added, "Do you want me to drive you? I switched out cars yesterday and put Carla back in the garage. I actually have my take-home vehicle today. How 'bout it?" She told him that would be nice as she grabbed a protein bar off the counter. He pointed to the stove and got her a plate down from the cabinet. He filled it with scrambled eggs, bacon, and an English muffin. "You have time to eat. Want a refill on that coffee?"

"What a nice surprise." He gestured for her to sit at the table. He offered her two Advil and a glass of water. After he made sure she took the pills, she sipped her coffee. She put her hand on his after she set her coffee down, "Thank you. It's been nice having you here with me." She began to eat her breakfast, "Calvin, you are such a great cook and you are spoiling me."

He gazed at her and replied, "I like spoiling you. Do you think you're going to be okay tonight or would you like me to come back?"

She glanced at him and didn't say anything. He reached out to capture her hand in his, "I'm not about to pressure you into something you don't want to happen. I want to be with you too much to ruin the relationship we have by being less than a gentleman." He loosened his hand from hers, "I can sleep in the guest room if you want me to come over tonight. Listen, you don't have to answer me now. Take the day and think about it. Text or call me when you decide, okay?" She nodded.

He watched her toy with the rest of her breakfast until he asked if she was ready to go. He told her he'd clean up the kitchen while she grabbed what she needed.

When they arrived at work, he parked in the Government Boulevard garage and waited. She glanced at him as he said, "Meeting today on your floor. Thought I'd ride up with you. That is if you don't mind sharing the elevator with your boyfriend." He tried to keep a straight face, but when she grinned, he couldn't help himself. He chuckled and put his hand on her back and walked with her to the elevator. When the doors opened, he walked in after her and was about to press the button when he heard someone ask them to hold the elevator. He obliged.

Noah Webster, The Public Safety Director, walked in and nodded to Calvin. He pressed the button for his floor and then looked at Lillette, "Well, good morning." She nodded, then looked away.

Calvin was standing close to Lillette and because he'd become accustomed to her body language, he wondered about the tension he felt in the air. Noah spoke again and aimed his question at the young woman standing next to the Police Chief, "So, did everyone have a good weekend?" He continued without waiting for a response, "I understand there was some trouble in your neighborhood. Hope everything turned out okay." He gave what Lillette could only describe as a smarmy smile.

Calvin took the reins of the conversation, "Yes, everything is fine." He turned to the woman he cared about and watched her fold her hands, but not before he saw the slightest tremor.

The director spoke up again, "That's good. That's really good. Lillette, I just want to let you know that what we talked about last time is still on the table."

The Chief of Police was about to say something when he heard the elevator ding. Noah spoke up with a smile, "Well, this looks like my floor. You all have a good day." The elevator doors stayed closed. At first the director looked puzzled, "The doors must be stuck. Lillette, would you be a doll and press that button again and see if we can get them open?" He was fixing the cuff of his suit jacket when he noticed the doors remained closed. Then he saw why. She had her finger on the button to keep them from opening. He asked, "Is there a problem?"

Calvin spoke up before she could, "What did you mean, Webster, when you talked about something still being on the table?"

He waved his hand in the air, "Oh, just business, right Lillette?"

Finally, she spoke, "You mean the last time we were on the elevator together and you made a pass at me? You told me if

51

I ever get tired of dating Calvin, that you'd make sure that you and I would have a good time together. You also made some dig about Calvin being older than me and wasn't it interesting that I picked him to date. Is that what you meant?" She turned to the man she was with and saw his expression cloud with outrage. "Chief, isn't that considered sexual harassment and aren't there strict policies about this in the workplace?"

The Director held up his hands, "Hey now, I was just making conversation. I can't help it if you took it the wrong way or read more into it than there was. Maybe the problem is with your interpretation." His eyes darkened with anger, "Anytime you want to talk about this further, I'll be more than happy to bring my lawyer into the equation."

The Chief of Police stood up straight with a commanding presence and said, "Yes, there are very strict guidelines for harassment." He gazed at the woman he cared for, "You are welcome to file a complaint, Lillette, any time you'd like. You are also welcomed to seek legal counsel. In fact, I know a great lawyer we can get clarification with if you feel the need to have any further information on the subject."

The Director of Public Safety let out a hiss and said, "If you will release the elevator button, I have a meeting."

"By all means," she answered as she let the button go and stood back so he could leave.

As Noah left the elevator and the doors closed behind him, Calvin turned to her, "If these cameras in this elevator weren't trained on us, I'd kiss the hell out of that pretty mouth of yours. You, Lillette Baker, are a badass!" They shared a laugh as he shook his head, then he got serious, "How come you didn't tell me the first time this happened?"

She pushed the button and the elevator began to climb, "It only happened the night of your birthday dinner. I was on the elevator trying to get home to get ready for our date. I thought he was an ass and wasn't going to say anything unless it happened again, which it just did. I can't believe he would flaunt his stupidity in front of you. I wasn't about to put up with that for a second time, although it did help having you here. Thank you."

The elevator opened, "Well, Chief Wynfrey, this is our floor. It's been an education." She glanced at him right before she got off and put her hand on the door, "By the way, I'm not the only badass around. My boyfriend happens to be one too." She winked at him when he smiled she said, "See you later."

He got off grinning. One of the secretaries saw the happiness on his face and remarked, "Something good happened I see."

He replied, "Oh, yes ma'am. You could say that." He opened the door to the conference room and began his day.


Noah Webster was seething by the time he reached his office. He put his work bag down and sat at his desk. He hit the contact on his burner phone. When the person on the other end answered, he said, "We have a problem and we need to take care of it now." He told the person on the line what just happened in the elevator with the Chief of Police and Lillette. "I can't help the fact that car didn't kill him. You want to wait that long? Fine. We'll wait. Yes, with the amount of people we are expecting, it would be easy to blend in with the crowd. Then it will be done and no one will be the wiser. I got it." After hanging up the phone, he stashed it back in his pocket to throw away later in the bay. He drummed his fingers on his desk. He got his keys out of his pocket and opened his desk drawer. Noah pulled out a picture of Lillette and muttered, "You just wait. You won't have your champion forever. Once he's gone, it's game on." He leaned back in his chair as a loathsome grin appeared on his face.

# Chapter 6

C alvin texted Lillette around lunch time to see if she wanted to meet downstairs at the new food court. He needed to stay close to the building but wanted to check on her to make sure she was okay. She texted back that she would meet him in a few minutes downstairs and was inviting her friend, Gavin, the lawyer, to be with them. He replied and hit the send button. When Calvin made his way to the brand new food court in the basement of the Government Complex, he saw that Gavin and Lillette were already waiting for him at a table. Gavin stood and nodded, "Chief."

Calvin bent over and kissed Lillette on the head, "Hey, glad you all could make it." As the Chief of Police was getting settled, the lawyer looked at his friend. She nodded her head and smiled. He took a deep breath and smiled as well. He was glad things were going well in their relationship. He would not hesitate to have a discussion with the Police Chief if they were not.

Gavin replied, "Yes, I understand there were some concerns about a certain elevator ride this morning. Anything I need to do?"

Lillette shook her head and put her hand on Calvin's, "I think he's not going to bother me anymore."

Her friend remarked, "You know, I think the Chief would agree with me that sometimes people who are obsessed have behavior that may escalate instead of leaving the object of their obsession alone."

Calvin frowned, "Yes, that has been known to happen."

She gave a short laugh and said, "Guys, I'm not about to walk on eggshells around here. I've been invaded in my home and insulted on the job. I'm done." She looked at the man she was falling in love with. She thought about that again. She had been in love with him for quite a while. She hadn't wanted to look at that before and she wasn't saying anything to him. Putting her hand on his she continued, "Calvin, I would like to get ahead of those defense training classes. I would feel safer if we could get that done."

He answered her, "I'll take care of that today."

Her friend joined in and added, "You could come to the gym with me and I could teach you how to box." Calvin looked intrigued so Gavin said, "You're welcome to come as well if you're interested."

At that moment, Lillette's phone buzzed, "Sorry, it's work." She looked at Calvin, "If you don't mind getting me a salad, I would appreciate it." She winked at him, "You know what I like." She smiled and moved away to take her call.

Gavin looked at him and gestured, "Shall we?" As they moved to the takeout counter to order salads, he glanced at the Chief of Police and remarked, "Things seemed to be going well. I haven't seen her this happy in a long time. I also appreciate you being there when that asshole attacked her at her house. He still in jail?"

"So far. It appears he was wanted in a carjacking that happened a couple of days ago along with assault and battery of his mother. She finally decided to press charges." He shook his head in disgust, "I think he's going to be a guest of ours for a while."

The lawyer and Calvin got the lunches and headed back to the table. They sipped their teas and waited for her. Gavin began, "As one of her oldest friends, I'll come right to the point. What are your intentions towards her? I don't want her hurt. I know her well and I'm betting because of your history, she hasn't said anything." The Chief looked up as Gavin continued, "She's in love with you." He watched the other man lower his drink and fold his hands on the table. He continued, "You didn't know that? She practically glows around you and when we talk your name comes up several times. I want her to have a happy life. She deserves it."

Before Calvin could say anything, Lillette returned. She took a deep breath, sipped her tea, and asked, "So, what did I miss?"

The two men looked at each other as Calvin said, "We were just trying to firm up a time to go boxing."

She took a bite of salad and replied, "Can't wait." She grinned at her friend, "Gavin, I'm up for the challenge. Just let me know when." She sipped her tea and ate her salad.

Gavin glanced at the Chief, "Yes, hopefully our Chief here is up for the challenge as well." Calvin gazed at the lawyer as they both knew he was talking about more than a workout. He was protecting Lillette and making sure Calvin understood that.

Calvin nodded his head, put his hand on hers and replied, "Yes, I'll be right by her side." Gavin chewed his salad, satisfied to hear his answer and smiled.

Night had fallen when Lillette answered her door and let Calvin in, "Maybe I just need to give you a key." She walked into his arms and held him; grateful he would be staying another night. She thought she had shaken off having her home invaded. She kept looking over her shoulder when she was in her backyard and hated feeling that way.

He spoke up, "I have a surprise for you. Close your eyes."

"Okay, since it's you, not a problem." She closed her eyes and felt something cold being placed in her hands.

"Okay, you can open them," he said.

"You did not! So, she already has the Moon pie Ice Cream out?" Lillette turned the ice cream in her hand from one of the oldest ice cream shops in the city. She pulled him in for a hug holding on to the ice cream before she held it to his cheek. She laughed and quickly pulled the carton back.

"Now, that's not funny. I do something nice for you and I get a freezer burn. You think you're cute, huh?" He advanced towards her as she turned and ran to the kitchen.

She looked around and found herself cornered. She held up the ice cream, "You better watch it. I have a deadly weapon." She grinned as he stalked towards her. She tucked the carton behind her on the counter. She closed her eyes and braced herself for what he would do to get back at her. He reached for the container behind her back and her body collided with his, her eyes flying open and meeting his, their game of cold revenge forgotten. Her hands were on his back and his arms were wrapped around her. She whispered his name and then his mouth was on hers and she held on, loving him, and feeling safe from harm from any threats of home invasion or harassing colleagues. Her heartbeat quickened and the kiss intensified. Because he had been tenderhearted and caring with her, she felt secure in moving her hands and gliding them over his muscular chest and his shoulders. His mouth shifted and moved up her neck, his fingers threading through her long chestnut hair.

He breathed her name, "Lillette," then he whispered in her ear, "tell me what you want. I love being close to you, but I'm not about to do something you're not ready for." He reined kisses up her cheek and his hands drifted down her shoulders. He held her as he felt her trembling in his arms. He whispered again, "Tell me."

It all came flooding back to her. She remembered the sensations and feelings between them. She craved his touch. If she was honest with herself, she wanted that again with him. This time, though, the stakes were so much higher. She desired considerably more than just a night and a morning. A future with him was what she wished for. She longed for marriage and a family with him. Lillette had found her life. She wondered now if his heart belonged to her. The words came tumbling out, "Calvin, at New Year's I wanted you. Now, I want us. It's a lot to ask when two people haven't been together for very long, but I want you as the partner I can love and who will love me for the long term. That means a commitment for life. That's what I wish for. That's what I need." Emotion clogged her throat as she waited for his response.

He leaned back to gaze into her eyes, "Lillette, I want…" A cell phone chirped loudly in his pocket. Taking a deep breath, he put his hand on her cheek, "It's my work phone. It might be an emergency." She nodded her head as his arms dropped from hers, "Yes. What?! What do you mean he's dead?" His eyes crawled up to hers, "What happened? Yes, Mr. Mayor, I'll be right there. Yes, I'll bring her with me." He turned to put his phone on the counter and held her hands, "Noah Webster is dead." He tightened his hold on her hands as she gasped. "They reviewed all the camera feeds in the building and happened to view the one of all three of us having a discussion on the elevator. They thought our body language was interesting. We've been called in to talk to the mayor and to Mack."

She took a shaky breath and spoke up, "Mack, The Assistant Chief of Police?"

"Yes." He pulled her forward and hugged her, preparing her for what he had to tell her.

Before he could say anything, she began to talk. "Can you tell me what happened?" she asked.

"He was found in his office with a letter opener driven through his heart." He took a breath and rubbed a hand over his head.

She shuddered, "Did they find any clues? Who could have done this?"

"I need you to call Gavin right now. Don't wait," he said.

"Gavin? What's he got to do with anything? Calvin, I don't understand…." And then it clicked as her face paled, "What else did they find and what does it have to do with me?"

He took her face in his hands. His Lillette was in for a fight, but he'd be by her side the whole time. There was no way someone was going to blame her for Noah's death. He'd move heaven, hell and all the contacts he had to make this right, "Listen to me, okay? You are to say nothing until Gavin is by your side. Do you understand? Say nothing."

"Calvin, you're scaring me. What did they find?"

He kissed her forehead and said, "It was a letter threatening to kill him if he didn't stop harassing you." He pulled her into his arms and he took a breath and continued, "It was signed by you." He heard her breathe heavily and then he finished it, "The letter opener that killed him has your fingerprints on it."

# Chapter 7

I t was almost the end of February, which meant it was Carnival Time. Mardi Gras was just beginning in certain cities in the state of Alabama. It was a busy time with crowds numbering in the thousands. Baldwin County was host to several parades but did not have the schedule of the bigger parades like the city across the bay. This allowed for a special couple to exchange their vows in a small venue overlooking the delta on the last Saturday of the month. The wedding party consisted of the bride and groom and their mothers. The couple insisted on a private ceremony for the wedding. The weekend before, the couple had a surprise engagement party hosted by the two mamas at Swanson's, an elegant restaurant owned by the Swanson family in Fairhope, Alabama. Just about all their friends and families were in attendance. Gary Rogers, Georgia's neighbor, was joined by his son and daughter-in-law. A young rookie officer was there to honor his mentor. A 14-year old girl named Danny took part as a guest and was escorted by Marlena and Dr. George Huntington. Leslie Sternum felt safe in coming to the dinner even though she was a few days overdue in having her baby. Her husband, Wally, her best friend Henry, and her parents, friends and family were right by her side. She had Hunt looking out for her just in case. The men and women who worked at the Bookworm took part in the festivities. The guests ate dinner, sipped champagne, and danced throughout the evening.

At one point, the announcer tapped on the bandstand. He introduced the couple and told the crowd the story of a young widow expecting a baby and the detective who fell in love with them both. The couple was asked to the center of the dance floor. The detective got down on one knee and held out a family heirloom. He proposed to the woman he loved. With tears in her eyes, the young woman accepted the proposal and the ring. The couple danced to an old Etta James song as the mamas looked on with tears in their eyes. The soon-to-be man and wife kissed when the song was over and everyone clapped for them. They received a variety of gifts for themselves and the baby.

Since their engagement party was such a huge affair, they decided the wedding should be just for immediate family. The detective was handsome in a navy suit with a yellow striped tie. The bride was elegant in a tea-length cocktail dress the color of lemons that enhanced her lush maternal figure. Drew couldn't take his eyes off her. The minister arrived at the wedding venue and began the ceremony. The couple said their vows and then when the minister declared them man and wife, they kissed and then held each other. A photographer captured the special moment and even took pictures of the wedding party outside the deck overlooking the delta and the bay. Their mothers hugged them both. After a celebratory lunch, the mothers said goodbye to their children. Since this was considered the weekend of the second parade on the island, there was not a Mardi Gras event scheduled Downtown. The detective drove up to the hotel and retrieved their suitcase and garment bag from the trunk.

After handing his keys to the valet, he spoke to his wife, "Happy Wedding night, Georgia Wynfrey Myers." He took her hand and led her into the hotel. Once things were situated at the front desk, the husband and wife took the elevator to their floor. As they reached their room, Drew turned to Georgia, "I love you. After our baby is born and it's safe to do so, I'll pick you up and carry you over the threshold to our home and we will celebrate another night together. But for now, welcome to our room." The door opened and Georgia was entranced. She spied the bottle of champagne chilling in the bucket with a tray of cheeses, fruit, and a small chocolate cake for them to share. She picked up the card and smiled. She showed it to Drew who said, "Those mamas sure are something else."

After touring the room, Georgia spoke up, "Oh, Drew, the bathroom is sheer heaven. I wouldn't mind a soak later in that wonderful bathtub, but you'll have to help me in and out." She glanced at the small step up to the tub. It would be a little bit of a challenge to get in and out of the tub, but she knew her husband would be right there to make sure she and the baby were safe, as he had done all along since being in their lives.

They explored the room further and she was excited at the fact that there was a coffee bar in the room, until she looked at the packets of decaf coffee and teas. There was a card there too. She read it aloud, "From your loving husband. I promise to give you the leaded version when allowed." Then she looked down at the bottom of the card. It said, "P.S. Because we are a team, I get the unleaded version as well. I love you and the little one." She smiled then moved over to give him a kiss.

He settled her in his arms and asked, "Hmm, what did I do to deserve that?"

"Well, that was a thank you for a wonderful two weeks. The engagement party and the wedding were just perfect. I've got mixed feelings about Calvin and Lillette not being able to join us for either event. I'm glad we've made our peace with him and I just adore her. She's a sweet young woman. Can you tell me what's going on there? Calvin really didn't say much. Just that there are some legal issues they are working through and he was sorry they couldn't be there for our special events."

Drew kissed her on the top of the head and replied, "My understanding is that there was someone high up in the city department that was murdered. They think Lillette is the key to solving the case. That's all Calvin told me. He said he might run some theories by me. They are frowning on him being involved because of his relationship with her. He told me he wasn't budging from her side." He grinned and hugged his wife, "He also said he told them he would divulge certain information if they asked him to step down, so they backed off." He shook his head and gave a short laugh, "He also told me he was bluffing, but they don't know that. Must be something there for him to find since they left him alone."

She reveled in her husband's embrace, "I hope it works out for them. I really do. I think Lillette has been good for Calvin and I think he finally understands what a valuable relationship he has with her. I wouldn't be surprised if they got married. I hope so. I'd like to see them as happy as we are." She gazed at the detective she fell in love with all those months ago.

He pulled her to him and hugged her, "Well, Mrs. Myers, I just have one question for you." She glanced at the merriment dancing in his eyes, "Do you need any help with getting comfortable? I didn't know if I needed to help you with your dress or anything else…" He couldn't finish as she put her fingers on his lips. He began to kiss her fingers one by one.

She looked at him and said, "Hold that thought." She picked up a small package and took it into the luxurious bathroom with her. Before she closed the door, she said, "I'll be right back. Would you like to pour us a little champagne?" She held up her fingers showing him how much she could have according to her new doctor.

Drew poured the champagne and said, "Are you hungry? We have a good assortment of fruit and cheeses." He was about to put an apple slice in his mouth when the bathroom door opened. As he turned, all his attention was focused on the vision of his wife in a blue sheer lace gown the color of the sky with a silky blue robe to match. He looked at her from head to toe. She was wearing a pair of clear small-heeled shoes. She was lovely and he was at a loss for words. He put down the apple slice as she sauntered across the room. His wife stopped right in front of him and began to take off his tie. She helped him with his jacket and began to unbutton his shirt. All he could do was just stare at her. She got his shirt off and dropped it on the nearest chair near the bed. His belt was next. He swallowed as she took that off and he finally found the words to say,

"Georgia, you are one beautiful woman and I am so glad we are husband and wife." He swept his hands down her arms and then held her hands. His mouth captured hers as he felt his pants hit the floor. He stepped out of them as he noticed it was her turn to look at him from head to toe. His heart raced. He gazed into her eyes as he said, "You seem to have me at a disadvantage. You still have your outfit on. As beautiful as it is on you, I was hoping you wouldn't mind taking it off." He took a deep breath as her hand moved to one of her straps. She slid it off her shoulder along with part of her robe and then stopped.

She turned her back to him, "I think I'm going to need a little help, if you don't mind detective, sir." She took a breath herself as she felt him slip off her robe from behind. His mouth moved to her shoulders as he kissed her there and trailed kisses up her neck as his fingers deftly pulled her straps down. The gown puddled at her feet. He took her hand and helped her as she stepped over the gown.

He led her to the bed and asked her to sit down. He kneeled on the carpet and ran his hand down her thigh to her calf then to her foot. He took off one shoe and began to knead her toes. He ran his hand up one calf and gently rubbed it. He then put his hand on her other foot and removed that shoe. He looked up into the eyes of his bride and realized she was breathing hard and waiting on him. Drew then took that foot in his hand and rubbed her instep, then worked his way up to the calf and then to her thigh. She was trembling, so he stopped the movement of his hands and helped her to stand. He then leaned over and flicked the covers down and helped her get comfortable in the bed. He joined her then pulled the covers up over them. They took their time loving each other that night as man and wife. Later that evening, room service was ordered. Drew dressed, met the server outside the door and wheeled the cart into the room himself. He glanced at his wife, who was gazing at her husband with love and desire, "Detective, your shirt is slightly wrinkled since I threw it on the chair. I'll have to apologize for that. You're always so neat and handsome."

He walked over to the bed as he unbuttoned his shirt and took it off, "I think I just solved that problem." He reached for her and kissed her on the head.

"Yes," she smiled as she kissed him on the lips, "You are very good at solving problems." Her eyes glistened as she looked at him, "I have a problem myself I hope you'd help me with tonight."

His eyes gleamed as he leaned over and kissed her, "What would that be?"

"For starters, you're too far away from me." He stretched out next to her under the covers. She took a breath, "That's better." She looked at him and then said, "You're still slightly dressed. Think you can help me solve that issue?" As Drew followed his wife's directions, she looked him in the eye and touched his shoulders, "I think you can probably figure out the rest on your own. You seem very intelligent."

He lowered his head and before his lips met hers, he said, "Yes, I'm very intelligent. I married you, didn't I?" Her hand cupped his cheek as he kissed her again and again.

Right before midnight, Georgia took Drew's hand as he helped her into the bathtub, "Be careful now," he said. The water was warm as she sank down under the bubbles. Her husband rolled a towel and put it behind her head. She was in heaven. Another hour went by and her husband again helped her by making sure she safely exited the tub. He wrapped a towel around her body and kissed her. Then he leaned down and kissed her stomach and was rewarded with a kick, "Well, someone's awake." He held his hand on her stomach and captured her mouth with his. He loved them both so much.

As she finished drying herself with the towel, he began to undress. He took the towel from her and hung it on the hook next to the shower. She looked at him with a question in her eyes as he remarked, "I'm going to take a shower." His eyes glowed as they swept over her body, her stomach round with a cherished life inside her. "I know you just had your soak, but I didn't know if you'd like to join me." She smiled and nodded. He opened the shower and held out his hand, "Careful, I don't want you to slip." He moved the bathroom rug over in front of the shower door. She took his hand and joined him.

Much later, dressed in comfortable robes provided by the hotel, the couple sat in bed and devoured the fruit and the small chocolate cake. Georgia remarked, "I thought I was full from lunch, but I managed to conquer that dinner we had earlier and this chocolate cake is pure sin."

He laughed and looked at his beautiful wife, "It is that." He took their empty plates and set them on the bedside table, "Do you want to know what else is pure sin?"

Her eyes glowed as she gazed at her handsome husband, "I have a feeling you're about to tell me."

She scooted down on the bed and turned towards him. He unbelted her robe, "You." He gazed down at her body and continued, "You are pure sin and I love every bit of you."

She kissed him and unbelted his robe, "Detective, I think you are overdressed for the occasion here. You don't mind if I help you, do you?"

His lips met hers in a gentle kiss as he replied, "I'm all about helping those in need and right now, I need you. So go ahead. Help me." He then grinned.

"Oh, there are those teeth again. Now, I know you really, really like me."

He held her and then before his mouth met hers said, "Georgia, I love you."

"The feeling's mutual. I love you too." The newlyweds took their time loving each other. The couple fell asleep holding one another, joy surrounding their hearts.

# Chapter 8

The next morning as he watched his lovely wife sleeping next to him, Drew realized how truly fortunate he was to be married to her. He quietly got up and ordered their breakfast. She was still sleeping when room service knocked on their door. He exchanged the cart from last night for the cart this morning. He set up the table in the room next to the window and opened the curtains but kept the sheers in place. He poured juice for her and set out the glasses of water. He took the fruit and cheese tray out of the small fridge in the room and placed it on the table. Then he made coffee. Drew walked over and the mattress dipped slightly as he lay down next to her, "Hey, good morning."

She stretched and opened her eyes. She smiled, "Good morning. Is that coffee I smell?"

He kissed her and replied, "I have a surprise for you, but it means getting out of this comfortable bed, putting on your robe and joining me." He kissed her again and she lovingly responded. He gently touched her stomach.

She stretched once more, "Just let me visit the bathroom and I'll join you." She took his hand as he helped her out of the bed. "Well, Drew, you got dressed again." Her gaze then followed his as she looked at the table set with their breakfast. She hugged him, "Oh, I see why now. Thank you. Breakfast is a wonderful surprise. Be right back." When she returned, he had changed back into his robe. He held out a chair for her as she smiled and kissed him. As she sat down, she waited for him before she drank her coffee. She took a deep breath and took that first sip. She held her cup and gazed at her husband who was smiling at her, "Drew Myers, is this what I think it is?"

He carefully clinked his cup to hers and replied, "Happy Honeymoon, Mrs. Myers. That leaded coffee is my wedding gift to you, but only one cup."

She stood up and hugged his neck, "Oh, thank you! Thank you!" She sat back down in her chair and sighed, holding the cup. He winked at her and began to eat his breakfast.

Since they had another night at the hotel, they showered and decided to take a walk Downtown. They visited art galleries, local shops and even browsed through a local produce market. Across from the market stood a majestic cathedral. The couple entered the massive doors in front and took a seat in a back pew. The solitude and quietness surrounded them. Drew looked to his right in his pew and found a bulletin that chronicled its history. A crypt for the burial of bishops was also a part of the church. He glanced towards the front where he saw a tight spiral staircase that led down to that area.

He leaned over to his wife and whispered, "Would you like to see the crypt?"

She looked at him with confusion, "There's a crypt in this church?" He nodded and pointed. She sat back in the pew and responded to her husband, "I don't think I would like to venture that far. I'm perfectly happy here." She grabbed his hand.

Love's Redemption

"Never thought I'd see the day when my tough Georgia was afraid to go down to see something like I just described." He squeezed her hand.

"I'm sorry, it just doesn't appeal to me at this time." She put her other hand on her stomach, "I wouldn't mind lighting some candles though and send up a prayer for Calvin and Lillette. I think they are going through a tough time. I'd like to also pray for the mamas. They are so good to us." He nodded as he followed his wife up the aisle to light several candles. She looked down at the spiral staircase as they passed it. He raised an eyebrow and she shook her head. He smiled and followed her out the door.

When they reached the hotel, they decided they'd like to tour the city a little more. With recommendations from the hotel, they called for their car and explored the Oakleigh Garden District. Drew parked the car at Washington Square and they took a walk around the neighborhoods. They'd worked up quite an appetite and their walk led them to an old Irish bar in one of the neighborhoods. Pushing the door open, Drew looked around for a table and his eyes landed on the couple in front of them, "Calvin?"

The man turned and replied, "Drew? Georgia? Well, I didn't expect you two over here. You had your ceremony yesterday. I thought you'd be over the bay." He shook his hand and then he took his sister-in-law's hand in his, "Hi. How are you doing?"

Georgia responded, "Hello, Calvin." She looked at the young woman, "Hello, Lillette. It's nice to see you both." Georgia noticed the dark circles under her eyes. She knew something was wrong. Maybe they could help.

Calvin had his hand under Lillette's elbow as she moved forward and said, "Hello Drew. Hello Georgia." Just then a waitress came forward and let them know that the only table available was up the steps in the next room. The foursome decided to dine together.

As they settled at the table, the waitress left to get their drinks. Drew spoke up, "Our mothers gifted us with a couple of nights at the hotel downtown. We got there yesterday."

Calvin responded, "We are sorry we couldn't be at the wedding, but congratulations." He looked over at Lillette, "Since it's your honeymoon, how about we treat you to lunch today?" She showed a small smile and nodded.

His sister-in-law spoke up, "Oh, you two don't have to do that."

Lillette spoke up, "Oh please. We'd like to."

Georgia and Drew smiled as they held hands. After ordering their meals, Drew asked, "So, do you two want to talk about anything? I understand there are some concerns." He looked at his wife, "Is there anything we can do to help?" They watched Lillette bite her lip and reach over for Calvin's hand.

The waitress brought the food to the table. When she left, Calvin put his arm around his companion, "After we eat, how 'bout we all take a walk?" The newlyweds nodded their heads and tucked into their meal.

After lunch, the couples walked to the park. Standing by the fountain, Lillette began to speak. She told the couple what happened in the elevator, talked about Noah Webster's death and the suspicions that had been cast over her. Calvin took it from there, discussing how bad things looked, but it was an ongoing investigation. A handwriting expert had been called in to review the letter that was allegedly written and signed by her. There was talk about the letter opener that also contained her fingerprints. No arrests had been made, although the mayor was pushing hard to wrap up the case. Her lawyer and friend, Gavin, was pushing back just as hard. Calvin was doing everything he could to uncover evidence to keep her from being blamed for the death. While Drew and Calvin put their heads together, Georgia and Lillette took a walk on the path surrounding the fountain.

The bookstore owner voiced her concern, "If you want to talk about anything, I can be a good listener." She looked at Drew and continued, "My husband has helped me so much and from the interactions I see with you and my brother-in-law, I see he is helping you too."

"I appreciate that, Georgia. Yes, Calvin has been my rock. He's been wonderful. My friend, Gavin, is a pro at being a defense attorney, so between the two of them, I feel safe. We've been over this a million times. I have no idea who would be setting me up."

Georgia asked, "Is there anyone who knows about your discussion on the elevator with Calvin and Mr. Webster?"

She shook her head, "I don't know. I get along with everyone at work. I didn't like Noah. There was just something smug and condescending about him. He asked me out several times and he just made me feel uncomfortable. I always told him I had work to do and couldn't go out with him. I don't think he bought that answer, but I wasn't about to date him." She shrugged, "Maybe he told someone about me and that got someone thinking. Maybe there's something sinister going on and whoever it is thinks I know something. I don't know anything."

Georgia patted her arm, "You have many friends, including us, so if you ever need to talk, you now have my number."

"I appreciate that." Lillette looked around, "Listen, we need to get you two back to your honeymoon. Once that baby is born, it's going to be all hands on deck, isn't it? You two need time to yourselves."

"Do you mind if I give you a hug?" asked the bookstore owner.

Lillette put her arms out and she was enveloped in a hug and got kicked for her efforts, "Oh my goodness, that little one's got some kick." They both laughed and walked over to the gentlemen deep in discussion. "Calvin, we need to let these two get back to their honeymoon. It was so good seeing you."

The honeymooners watched the couple walk down the sidewalk. Drew was the first to speak, "Did you come up with anything when you ladies were talking?"

She shook her head, "No, did you?"

"Well, there are a couple of theories, but nothing solid." He kissed the top of her head, "You ready to head back?" He turned to his wife and took her face in his hands. He kissed her then said, "I have a surprise for you. I hope you like it."

She grinned, "So far detective, I've liked everything I've seen." She gazed at him from head to toe.

"Oh, Georgia, you sure know how to make a man feel like a king. The surprise this afternoon doesn't include me." She raised her eyebrow and he responded, "You'll see. My involvement with you comes later." He smiled as he took her hand to help her into the car. When they reached the hotel and the valet secured their car, he took her up to the spa. He kissed her hand and then kissed her on the forehead, "My dear wife, this is part of our Happy Honeymoon." A lady greeted them at the desk. Drew kissed her once more and hugged her, "Text me when you're ready and I'll come meet you right here."

"Drew Myers, I love you. Thank you." As the lady began to lead her away, Georgia winked at her husband and said, "See you later."

He nodded and walked down to the hotel bar. He ordered a beer and tucked himself at a table that gave him a view of the room and the doors leading in and out. He chuckled to himself and thought, "Once a cop, always a cop." The waitress delivered a bowl of pretzels and his beer. He got comfortable, sipped his drink, and divided his attention between a movie and a basketball game. After about an hour, he let himself into their room. He just noticed it had been straightened, so he ducked into the bathroom and saw they had placed new towels in there. Sauntering back into the main room, he spied a card propped against the champagne bucket along with a new bottle of champagne. Opening the card, Drew began to read aloud, "To Drew and Georgia, have a great honeymoon. From Calvin and Lillette." Drew then held up a gift certificate good for dinner for two in the restaurant across the street, "Well, I'll be." He then looked at the brochure attached that showed a restaurant with a panoramic view of the city and the bay. He then looked over at his rumpled dress shirt on the chair and said to himself, "Well, I'd better get to work if we are going to look good for dinner."

He glanced at Georgia's yellow dress hanging up in the closet and then began to get out the ironing board and iron.

An hour later, Drew got off the elevator at the spa. His wife greeted him with a relaxed look about her and a big smile. She hugged him, "I had such a great time. I got a special massage from a lady who knows how to work with pregnant women. They served me chilled water and a small charcuterie tray. I read two magazines, then closed my eyes. It was pure heaven." She glanced at him as they reached the elevator, "What did you do with your time?" He told her about his visit to the bar and that they had a gift that had been delivered to their room. Georgia was surprised when she reached their room and found out where they would spend their evening.

Dressed for dinner, the newlyweds got off the elevator and stepped into an elegant restaurant on the top of a 34-story building. Drew followed his wife, with a hand to the small of her back. They were seated right next to the window and had an eye view of the city. Over dinner, the couple in love enjoyed their meal and their conversation. There was a jazz band playing so Drew asked his wife for a dance. Holding each other closely, the detective and the bookstore owner moved around the dance floor slowly, enjoying the night. At one point, they stopped to take in the view. Full from dinner, the couple declined dessert. Holding hands, they made their way back to their hotel room. He brought her hand up to his mouth and kissed it, "Well, Mrs. Myers, how did you like the restaurant?"

Georgia replied, "Oh, husband of mine, it was just great." She smoothed her hand over her stomach as she felt a kick, "Our child agrees." She stopped on the sidewalk next to the hotel as Drew put his hand on top of hers and felt another kick.

He leaned down and whispered in the vicinity of her stomach, "Hey, kiddo. Not so rough on your mama, okay?" He kept his hand on her stomach and felt a calmness and smugly declared to his wife, "See, he or she is listening to me already." He felt his eyes moisten, "Oh, I can't wait, Georgia. I promise to you and the little one that I'll try my hardest to be the best dad I can be for our child."

His eyes weren't the only ones that had watered. "I love you. I know you'll be a great dad. We're both looking forward to that." Their hands still touching on her stomach she spoke again, "Now, how about we call it a night and make our way to our room? I'm ready to be loved on by my man." Her eyes met his and he smiled.

"Bookworm, you've got yourself a deal." He followed her into the hotel. When the elevator doors closed, he leaned over and kissed her, "I love you, Georgia Myers." As the doors opened, they walked to their room.

He opened the door and once inside watched his wife gaze at him. "I love you too," she said. Locking the door, he turned back to her and took her into his arms.

# Chapter 9

February was not only a special month for newlyweds, but for new parents as well. A stormy day did not dim their joy when Adelia June Sternum arrived into the world with a lusty cry to let everyone know that she was here at last. The proud dad leaned over the hospital bed and kissed his wife with tears in his eyes as the nurse settled their baby on Leslie's chest. She said through her own tears, "Adelia, we are so glad you're here." Wally bent down and gently kissed his daughter's head then moved over to kiss his wife again. She put her hand on her husband's cheek and said, "Thank you." He turned his face to kiss her hand. She then whispered to their little girl, "Just wait until we get you home so you can meet Jethro. You're going to love living on the farm."

Wally smiled at his family and took a deep breath. He shook his head at the blessings that had come his way in the last year. Seeing where the blanket had revealed his child's feet, he touched her toes and grinned at their little girl's mama. He spoke up, "Hey, I'm going to go get our visitors who are waiting to meet our Adelia." Wally choked up as he spoke her name. He wiped his eyes and walked out of the room. He immediately was spotted by both sets of parents along with Curtis and Karen.

Leslie's best friend, Henry, was there as well with Jeff. After being hugged by all, he said, "Okay, there's limited room, so they told us only a few family members at a time." Wally looked at the excitement on the grandparents' faces and waved them on into the room.

The proud father looked down as a plush stuffed cow was thrust into his hands. Curtis cleared his throat, "This is a gift from our theme park friends. Florence thought since Adelia would be living on a farm she needed to begin learning about farm animals." Curtis grinned and put his arm around his wife.

An envelope was then handed to Wally. He looked up at Henry and Jeff, who were smiling. Henry said, "This is her first savings bond. I'm sure there will be many more to come."

Leslie's best friend's eyes moistened as Jeff took a step forward holding a large, wrapped package. He handed it to the new father and said, "I know Leslie has purchased art from my Mardi Gras Collection. This is my latest and thought we'd get Adelia started with her own collection. I thought you and Leslie would like to open it together."

Wally clasped Jeff's shoulder, "Thank you." He looked around at the group before him, "Our daughter is a lucky girl to have all of you." He gave a short laugh, "I have a feeling she's going to be incredibly spoiled."

Karen chimed in, "Just think, when she's a teenager, we can drink coffee together and I can teach her all about my special blends."

Adelia's father smiled and said, "Maybe she and I can always stop by your house after we go running."

Henry replied with a laugh, "Don't you worry. Uncle Henry can also help take care of keeping her active. She'll be a black belt in no time."

Curtis chuckled, "Just think, between helping on the farm, learning how to run a business and staying active, she's going to be one smart and talented girl." Wally couldn't agree more.

A few days later, Leslie was settling in their home with the new addition to the family. She was comfortable in the brand new rocking chair that was a gift from Edward and Janet. Leslie's mother and Wally's mom worked together to cook a big Sunday dinner. Curtis had his arm around Karen as they admired their brand new niece, who was currently being held by Owen, Leslie's dad. Wally loved his little girl. It was evident for all to see by the constant smile he had on his face. While everyone was admiring the new baby, Wally and his dad took Jethro for a walk. Wally, Sr. turned to his son, "Well, I have to say, I never thought our little girl would get here. Your mom and I are just so excited. We are so proud of the man you've become and of your family."

"Thanks Dad. It seems so surreal. I can't believe she's here either. It seems like yesterday I let Leslie into my world." He laughed, "I'll say that again, when Leslie barreled into my world." He smoothed his hair back with his hand, "I just really never saw her coming. She was relentless in trying to make me see how much we needed each other." He glanced at his dad, "I never thought I deserved her. Sometimes, I still don't think I deserve what I have. I think about what June's parents won't have since they lost their girls."

His dad stopped and turned to him, "I know you won't forget your first wife, June. She was your first love and you had a great marriage. I'm happy you'll keep her in your memory. She was a wonderful daughter-in-law and your mother and I loved her. When she lost her life, I didn't think we'd ever reach you again. It's like you died when she did." Wally crossed his arms and looked out over the vast fields of the family farm. His dad continued, "We were so moved when you used June's name for our granddaughter's middle name. Did you talk to her parents?"

Wally took a breath, "I called Mr. Gaines and we talked for a while. He was happy. Then Mrs. Gaines got home in time to talk to me too. They wanted to thank us for honoring June. They were even more surprised when I told them it was Leslie's idea." Wally and his dad began to walk again with Jethro in tow. He continued, "They're coming for a visit soon for the quarterly board meeting for the Center, so they'll be over for dinner if you and mom would like to see them. You are more than welcome. We'll let you know soon when we get it all together for their visit."

Father and son walked a few minutes in companionable silence, when his dad asked with a short laugh, "So, anyone have a nickname for my granddaughter yet?"

Wally grinned as he replied, "Well, I called her 'Addy' at midnight last night trying to rock her back to sleep. Leslie likes to sing out, 'Adelia Dear' when she's crying and goes to pick her up from her bassinet." He shook his head when he heard what his father-in-law called her and grimaced, but then laughed, "And of course, Owen has already christened her with the name 'Dilly Pop'. Abby calls her, 'Adelia, My Sweetie.' He cleared his throat, "God love her teachers when she starts school. She'll be so confused about what her name should be. He then glanced at his dad, "Well, when am I going to hear from you and Mom? What's going to be the nickname from you all?"

His dad's eyes twinkled with merriment when he replied, "You'd never speak to us again if I told you."

Wally huffed out, "Oh, come on. Can't be that bad." He looked at his father's happy face then thought about it again, "I don't think I want to know. My mother has a wicked sense of humor and you're no better." He took a deep breath and closed his eyes, "Okay, let me have it."

Wally, Sr. looked at his son and said, "We thought we'd call her 'Adda Girl'. Just think she'd have praise from us all the time. 'Adda Girl', you're doing great. 'Adda Girl', Grand-Pere and Grand'Mere just love you. So, what do you think?"

His son opened his eyes, stared at his father, and abruptly turned down the path with Jethro to walk back home. He kept going even when his father burst out laughing and jogged to catch up with him. He put his hand on his son's arm until he stood still. He hugged his son and ruffled his hair, "I had you going good, didn't I?" His father continued to laugh, "Just priceless. You're face. If you could have seen your face. I just couldn't help myself." Laughing again, he cupped his son's cheek, "Your mom and I are so happy that you have a little girl." The laughter died down as his eyes moistened. He clasped his boy's shoulder, "If you and Leslie don't mind, we'd like to call her June Bug. We just love her so much. Would you be okay with that?"

Wally rubbed his eyes and pulled his father in for a hug, "Dad, we'd love it. She is going to be such a well-loved baby."

He let go of his father as they reached the front yard. As they began to walk into the house, he looked over at his dad, "Good Lord, I thought you were serious wanting to call her 'Adda Girl'. You and my mother are so twisted. I don't know how I made it through my teenage years without having some serious hang ups." Laughter rang out behind him as his dad followed him into the house.

When the doorbell rang later that afternoon, Abby went to answer and saw the artist who rented the old farm house from them and a nice looking young man at the door. "Well, Effie, how are you? Everything okay with the house?"

Effie walked in and everyone knew her from being around the farm, "Yes, ma'am, the house is great." She looked to her companion and then to the family gathered in the living room, "This is Gavin. I wanted you all to meet him." The couple was welcomed and offered dessert and coffee. Effie spoke up and looked at Gavin, as he nodded, "We would like to give Adelia a gift from us. We can even hang it if you like the piece." She watched as Leslie handed over the baby to Brenda, Wally's mother. Effie then handed over the wrapped art to Leslie. As the gift was opened and held up to the light, gasps were heard around the room.

The new mother was in awe, "Effie, oh my. Saying this is beautiful just doesn't do it justice." Leslie held the stain-glassed baby mobile up for everyone to see. A rainbow of colors reflected into the room. Effie was soon given a hug by Leslie. Wally walked over to thank them and asked if they would like to hold the baby. The artist headed to the kitchen to wash her hands. Then she walked back into the room and held out her arms and gently cradled Adelia. She looked up at Gavin and grinned. The newly arrived couple spent the next hour eating pie and helped to hang the mobile in the baby's room.

Saying their goodbyes, Gavin and Effie walked to the old farm house holding hands. He was the first one to speak, "You know, this is pretty convenient, all the families living close-by. We didn't even have to get in our cars to come here."

She agreed and replied, "You know, speaking of cars, don't you think it's time to get you a new one? That clunker you have has over 150,000 miles on it."

He replied, "Hey, don't speak ill of my old Honda. Many times, I have thought about our first date when I brought you home and we talked all night in my car. Don't you have fond memories of that night? I remember that we watched the stars from my sunroof and we slept together for the first time in that car."

Gavin was taken off guard when she glared at him and responded, "Yeah, you say that out loud when anyone else is around, you can certainly forget spending any more time with me. Nothing happened that night and you know it. We just slept and nothing else. I don't need people thinking I'm that kind of girl. I had enough of that in high school." She hurried her steps along as Gavin watched her. She continued talking, caught up in the past, "A bunch of mean girls spouting off stories about me just because I was shy, uncoordinated and an easy mark. Didn't stop them from spreading rumors about me sleeping around. Took my brother finding out who it was and calling them out. Told them if they ever bothered me again he'd call a meeting with all of their parents and invite the cops to press charges of harassment. Like I need to relive that." He put his hands in his pockets and came to a standstill.

She kept moving at a fast clip. She wound down and finally stopped with her hands covering her eyes in frustrated tears. After a few minutes, realizing she was alone she turned and saw his face. Effie ran back to him and he caught her with a muttered, "Oof!" when she barreled into him. She kept apologizing, "I'm so sorry! I'm so sorry! I know you would never do that. Sometimes I get caught up in the past and I really shouldn't let it bother me. It was a long time ago. I am so sorry." She took her time, but finally raised her face to his. The look of hurt was still there clouding his beautiful blue eyes, "Please Gavin, say something."

He put his hands into her hair and pulled her close. His mouth touched hers and she clung to him. When they finished that kiss, he continued, "Effie, your brother never shared that with me. I didn't know that. I'm sorry if I said anything wrong." He took a breath, "You are everything I have ever wanted in a woman. I'm well aware nothing happened, but I do have fond memories of holding you in that car all night long. It's what gets me through the tough times at work, especially when I have to go to bat for children and adults who have been abused or bullied out there in the world." He took a breath, "As a lawyer, I've seen some families go through the unimaginable." He took her in his arms and held her with his chin resting on her head, "You had a bad experience in high school. I do understand." He lifted her face with his finger under her chin, "But, Effie, don't ever make the mistake of lumping me in with what other people do. You know me." He kissed her on the forehead and continued, "The reason that I'm with you is because you ground me, Paris, and you make it even easier to get through those times when I'm working to help others." He held her at arm's length and stared into her eyes, "I love you, Effie. I have for a while now. I just didn't know how to say it to you."

She looked at him loving his nickname for her. He liked to call her Paris because she was named for the famous landmark. Her eyes bright with tears she murmured, "I think you did just fine." She put her hand on his cheek and touched his mouth with hers in a gentle kiss. Once she found her breath, she replied, "I love you too." The couple smiled at each other, holding hands, as they walked back to her house. She glanced over at the man she loved, "So, what do you want to do with the rest of our evening?" She sighed and even felt her heart melt when she saw his grin. She responded, "Oh, Gavin, whatever am I going to do with you?"

When they got to her front door he bent down and whispered in her ear, "What are you going to do with me?" His eyes sparkled with mischief, "Darlin' whatever you want. I'm yours." She hit his arm playfully and laughed as the door shut behind them.

Her eyes twinkled as she tossed a look over her shoulder, "Well, I do have something I'd like you to do with me." His eyes widened and he grinned.

An hour later, Effie admired her toes, "Well, Gavin Jackson, if you ever get tired of being a lawyer, you could always work in a spa. I appreciate what you just did with my toes."

He smiled and gazed at her with a rapt expression in his eyes, "I'd rather do something else than just giving you a pedicure. Kissing you does come to mind." He noticed her take a deep breath, a smile reaching her eyes. Looking back at her toes, he huffed, "After all, you're the artist here. I think you just keep me around for the free labor." He took a breath and looked at all the bottles of nail polish on the table, "I do like the red color. Makes your nails pop." He laughed, "Good Lord, not only do you have me painting your nails, but you've also got me spouting about what I see in those magazines in my outer office at work." He ran his hand under the bottom of her toes and smiled when he saw her shiver, "I have always been partial to red." He made a point of looking at her red hair and then moved his gaze all the way down to her feet. A grin bloomed on his face.

She laughed and corrected him, "I beg to differ. That color is not red. It's called *I'm Not Really a Waitress*." She glanced over at the variety of colors, "It's actually my favorite."

She watched as he picked up the bottles and read the bottom of each one, "*Cajun Shrimp, She's a Bad Muffuletta, How to Jamaica Million, You're a Pisa Work...* My mother used to paint her nails and all I remember is red and pink. Nail polish has come a long way." He smiled. He looked further down the table and saw a box shaped like the Eiffel Tower, "Ok, Paris, what's in the tower?"

Pausing in the act of straightening the nail polish, she looked over her shoulder, "That is from my grandmother. You remember, the one who went to Paris and convinced my parents to go along with my career as an artist?" He nodded and then she said, "They had a French Collection in that brand that she gave me." She carried the box over to the kitchen counter and motioned with her head for him to join her, "Now, this is a very special container and it carries a very special collection." She batted her eyelashes at him, "And I only let people I really care about know what's in here."

Gavin winked and cleared his throat then whispered, "Paris, I think you're secret is safe with me." He looked around as if to make sure no one else was in the room and crossed his heart with his finger, "I promise to never utter a word about what I have seen here today." Then he raised his hand, "Scout's Honor." His mouth twitched and his eyes sparkled.

"You know, you can be a smartass when you put your mind to it. Well, I'll just take my tower of polish and put it away." She reached for the container and he stopped her by taking her hand.

He shook his head, "Not just yet. I deserve to see what's in the tower since I painted those toes. You owe me. Now, out of the way, Paris."

She stared at him and he didn't flinch. She took a breath, "Fine." She moved out of the way.

He stepped up, opened the container and whistled. He began to pick up each bottle and read the label on the bottom, "*Louvre Me Louvre Me Not, Tickle My France'y, I'm Fondue of You, Bastille My Heart, Yes…I Can-Can and We'll Always Have Paris.*" Gavin put each bottle back in the container. "Paris, I have to admit, this may beat out my baseball card collection." He stepped back as she eyed him, then carried her Tower Box and backed out of the room, staring at him the whole time. Once she left the room, his mouth curved into a smile, then a grin. He leaned his arms on the counter and began to laugh, "Oh that was priceless." He cleared his throat and stood up as she came back into the room, trying to keep a straight face and failing miserably.

Effie walked right up to him and asked, "So, are you cooking me supper too?"

He pulled her into his arms, "As long as you don't mind me making myself at home, going through your cabinets and your fridge." He kissed her on the nose, "I mean it is your house and you're the boss. Wouldn't want to step on your toes or anything." He smirked as he looked down at her bare feet and honed in on her toes.

She pulled her head up and kissed him, "Thank you for painting my toes and feeding me tonight. Maybe I'll return the favor one day."

He pulled her into him, his hands loosely hugging her waist, while she mirrored his movements. He kissed the top of her head then replied, "I'm okay on the food making, but the toe dressing up, that's all you." Letting her go, he rubbed his hands together, "Now let's see what you have in this fridge."

An hour later, their empty dishes told the tale of satisfaction. Sipping a beer, Effie murmured, "Oh, Gavin Jackson, you sure are full of surprises. Crawfish Jambalaya. Oh my."

"Yeh, it was a nice surprise what you had in your freezer." He looked over at her counter, "And the fresh produce came in handy. Those tomatoes are out of this world."

She leaned back in her chair, sated from his culinary masterpiece, "The Daltons keep me stocked with fresh veggies. I'm very lucky to live here. By the way, thank you again for cooking."

He glanced her way, "Anytime Paris."

Her eyes met his, "So, you have to go soon?"

He gave her a sizzling look and thought he wouldn't mind kissing her sweet mouth. Gavin took a breath, "I do have court in the morning. What'd you have in mind?"

Thirty minutes later, with the dishes cleaned, settling in the drying rack on the counter, Gavin was once again holding a bottle of nail polish, "How is it, Effie, that we just didn't do fingernails and toes at the same time?"

With humor showing in her eyes, she said, "I don't know. Just wasn't feeling it then. But, with your choice of culinary Cajun tonight, I thought I'd bring out my New Orleans collection. Look on the bottom."

Gavin read the tiny label, *"Crawfishin' for a Compliment,"* He laughed, "Cute, Paris."

"Now read the other one," she said as she handed him another bottle.

*"Got Myself Into A Jam-Balaya."* He just shook his head and smirked, "Very appropriate." He raised his eyebrow and looked at her feet, "You know, neither one of these colors match what you've got on your toes. Aren't they supposed to match?" he asked.

She shook her head and grinned, "Not necessarily, Perry Mason." She sat at one of the barstools around the kitchen island and held her hands out, "Anytime you're ready lawyer man."

The man who defended many a client, wore suits to work, and was a Master of Law in the courtroom, plopped down on a stool and gestured for her to move closer. He took her one hand in his and both bottles of polish in his other hand, "Okay, Paris, pick your poison and prepare to watch how a genius in the art of nail technique operates."

She couldn't stop the snicker from escaping her mouth. He raised one eyebrow at her response and she bit her lip from smiling. As the man she loved painted her nails, she swallowed a bubble of happiness. She could no more stop the smile from blossoming on her face than she could stop the sun from rising. He looked up and took in her radiant expression, then winked at her and got back to work.

# Chapter 10

C alvin was extremely busy with the Mardi Gras parade schedule. Carnival time was late this year due to where it fell on the calendar. In between his time at the office and riding in the police car for the parades, he saw Lillette when he could. Gavin and she would meet him for an early dinner. Then he was swallowed up in his duties during Carnival. The Sunday after the first full week of Mardi Gras gave them both a break. Calvin was invited over for a homemade brunch prepared by the woman he loved. Then they broke out the fire pit that afternoon, moved a couple of chairs closer to the fire and just talked. She was comforted by the flames flickering in the backyard and by him. She could get through anything with him by her side. She held his hand then when she could no longer hold in what she wanted to say, she spoke, "I want to go to New Orleans to see my aunts." When he frowned at her and opened his mouth to speak, she gripped his hand tightly and announced, "I need some time away from the city. As much as I love living here, I need to get away for a while." When his eyes moved away from hers, she moved over to sit on his lap, "Calvin, look at me Honey."

He gazed into her hazel eyes and she took a deep breath, "I love you. If you don't think those above you will think I'm a fugitive, I'm leaving town."

His heart turned over due to her declaration of love and because she was leaving, "You haven't done anything wrong. You haven't been charged with any crime. There is only circumstantial evidence." He held her tightly, savoring their time when he knew her leaving was the best thing for her. He couldn't take that from her. She'd been through hell.

Kissing him on the mouth, she exhaled, "You know it's not you. It's going to be so hard being away from you." Her eyes moistened, "I'll miss you."

He returned her kiss, his lips lingering on hers. He moved his hand under all her luxurious hair and caressed the back of her neck. Closing her eyes, she shivered at his touch. Before she knew what was happening, he stood them both up. She watched as her beloved police chief put his hands in his pockets and walked to her back fence, studying all the painted handprints that made the fence come alive with color and the innocence of children. When he asked her about the handprints the first time he visited her home, she told him she had invited all of the children in the neighborhood over to decorate her wooden fence. She explained that she had several trays of paint. The kids took turns holding out their hands and having each other paint their hands with a big paintbrush. Then they stuck their hands to a board on the fence to create their handprints. She considered the white boarded painted structure a masterpiece. Walking towards the man she loved with all her heart, she reached for his hand as she got closer and held on.

He squeezed her hand and grinned, "So, you still have young Charlie's handprint for all the world to see." Calvin laughed.

She chuckled, "Yes, seems unfortunate that he broke the one finger that's considered a universal symbol for some adults. When he told me his mom wouldn't mind if we painted over the bandaged dressing on his middle digit, I never knew that finger would really stand out and make a profound statement." She laughed and threaded her arm through his, "So, you okay with me heading out tomorrow?"

Calvin gazed at the woman who belonged to him and felt like the luckiest man on earth. He replied, "Yeah, everything's good. You spend time with your aunts." He ran a hand over his head, "From what you've told me about them, you should have a lively time." Smiling, he kissed her forehead and knew it was time to tell her how he felt about her, "I love you, Lillette Baker. Eat a beignet for me and have a cup of good coffee while you're there."

Their eyes met and they gravitated towards one another, arms reaching, and then holding on to each other, feeling the love they shared, "All right, now. One more kiss and I'm going to let you pack and rest up for your trip. I love you."

Her words back to him were muffled by her head burrowing into his chest, "I love you too." She raised her head as her eyes crawled to his, "Now, what can I bring you back home? Want a Saints hat or some pralines?"

She took a breath as his mouth lowered to hers. Before their lips met, he responded, "You." He then kissed her. When he could take a breath, he said, "I just want you back safe and sound and holding onto me."

"You got it Chief." She put her hand on his cheek, kissed him good night and walked him to the front porch. He waited until she was safely inside and walked toward his automobile, Carla, who was ready to take him home. Once behind the wheel, he thought of his Lillette. He wouldn't begrudge her time with her family. He missed her already. Glancing at her house one more time, he started the car and worked his way home.

# Chapter 11

New Orleans has always been considered a gumbo mix of neighborhoods, restaurants, and endless places to shop. As the Uber cruised through the Garden District, Lillette marveled at all the majestic homes. Stately mansions, beautiful gardens and shot gun houses stared back at her. Arriving at her destination on State Street, she thanked the driver, who helped her unload her suitcases. Rolling her two bags through the gate, she climbed the steps and the door was opened before she could ring the bell. Delight showed on her face as she was enveloped in a hug by her Aunt Genevieve, "LAWD child, you are a sight for sore eyes. It's about time you got here. Your Aunt Rowena has been on pins and needles all morning." She watched her aunt roll her eyes, "That is when she's not on that phone wheeling and dealing trying to entice people into buying houses or God forbid, condos." She laughed as her aunt shuddered.

Lillette hugged her aunt back, careful not to hug too hard, for she could tell her aunt had lost weight and seemed a little frail. Although her aunt would never admit the toll losing her husband had cost her, Aunt Genevieve was a character. Her husband, Bud, had passed away a year earlier. Aunt Rowena's husband, known to all as Uncle Siggy, had passed a few years back. So, the aunts decided it made sense to live together. She didn't know how it worked, but it did. Both women had huge personalities and were stubborn to boot but were successful in sharing the same house.

"Well, it's about time." Lillette looked up and spied her Aunt Rowena coming out of the kitchen, "I was just making some coffee when I heard Ginny's high pitched laugh." She pinched her nose, "It's enough to wake the damn neighborhood, not to mention those buried in St. Louis Cemetery." Her arms came around her niece.

"Damn Rowena, that's clear across Claiborne Avenue," muttered Genevieve.

"My point exactly Ginny. Your voice carries that far." She kissed her niece on the cheek and then moved her hands to rest on her own slim hips. Lillette followed her aunt's movement and hoped she could keep her figure when she got older like her aunts did. They always looked so polished. Rowena had darker hair that she always kept groomed with pencil thin eyebrows, giving her the air of a long-ago movie star. Genevieve had brunette short hair which had started showing signs of gray. Her face showed the wrinkles more than Rowena's due to the fact that her Aunt Ro had monthly beauty treatments, which she'd never talk about out loud. She scooted to the bathroom and let her aunts fuss over her by allowing them to unpack her suitcases and hang her clothes, all the while arguing about the best restaurant to have dinner with their niece. She heard snatches of conversation through the bathroom door about the comparison of Commander's Palace to Brennan's to Dooky Chase's.

Lillette bit her cheek to hold in her grin. If nothing else, it wouldn't be a dull vacation. She thought she'd intervene before the insults got worse. Opening the bathroom door, she said, "Ladies, Mom sent you a care package from Mobile. How about we get settled in the kitchen with coffee and you can open up your gift?" She ducked her head and grinned as she followed them out of the room, listening to them now debating whether Randazzo's, Brocato's or Haydel's made the best king cake. She watched as her Aunt Genevieve set out the coffee service with a small plate of amaretto cookies situated on the tray. Royal Doulton fine china held the coffee with chicory that was poured by her Aunt Ro. Her Aunt Ginny opened up the gift from her mom. It was two tickets to the Phantom of the Opera that would open at the Saenger next month. They both hugged her and told her they'd call her mom later to thank her.

Rowena looked at the china, "Ginny, I don't know why you continue to use my delicate dishes when we could use your Vintage Paragon Cups and Saucers with the floral pattern. They are better suited for our niece who we are trying to spoil here. No offense, Honey, but since I grew up in Mobile I know there are a few antique shops that carry fine china, but not like the shops on Royal Street." She took a breath and nibbled on a cookie and raised one dark pencil thin eyebrow, "We want to give you a nice experience while you're here, so using the other cups and saucers would have made for a better presentation." She glowered at Genevieve.

Her other aunt didn't back down, "Rowena, you try my patience sometimes, you really do. I'm not making use of what I like to think of as my earthenware because last time it was utilized, you broke a cup and saucer. As you claim to be an expert on anything antique, and no, I'm not referring to your age, but you should be more careful when handling my things. I had to dip into the oil money to replace that one cup and saucer. I swear."

Ignoring her sister, Rowena crossed her legs and raised an eyebrow, "So dear, tell us all about this young man of yours. Your mother says he's handsome, drives a Mustang and dotes on you."

Even though she was an adult, it still didn't stop the pink flush flooding her face. But then, the smile she couldn't contain was like the sun bursting from the clouds in the sky. "Well," Genevieve purred, "Let's get down to brass tacks. Start from the beginning and don't leave anything out." She sipped her coffee and added, "We're two doddering old ladies who need all the details of your romance, since we don't have men in our lives anymore." She glanced up at her sister, "Except for Rowena. Charlie Guidry, who's the senior manager of Rouses Grocery Store, always needs to help her when she's looking for produce. But I'm not complaining. The lettuce is always fresh, just like Charlie, right Ro?" Watching Rowena glare at Genevieve was a riot, and Lillette bit her lip so as not to laugh. It was going to be an interesting two weeks, that was for sure.

By mid-week, Lillette had settled into a routine. She stretched her arms back and forth as she walked down State Street. She passed a beautiful church and stately homes, although this street didn't boast the number of mansions located on other streets throughout the Garden District. It seemed like a quiet neighborhood with more modest homes. Picking up the pace, she reflected on her phone call with Calvin last night. After an afternoon and a quiet dinner at the house with the aunts, pleading exhaustion, Lillette had retired to her room for the evening. Lying in the antique bed, she spent almost an hour talking to the man she missed with all her heart. When had he become her life? She thought about where they had started with each other and where they were now.

It began as a roller coaster ride into a relationship she never thought she'd have with Calvin, especially how they started out together. Giving herself to him on New Year's Eve was one of the most brazen things she had ever done, and after it happened, she was ashamed of herself. Or so she thought. When she had explained that time to her friend Gavin, he had listened and helped her see that was life. After being angry on her behalf, he reminded her she was a wonderful woman who any man worth his salt should treat with respect. Her brother's best friend then went on to explain that he was confident she would find the man she needed and wanted. After giving Calvin a second chance, their relationship had exceeded her expectations. Most of the friends her age were already married, many of them with children. That was okay. She loved her friends and couldn't compare her life to theirs. Remembering their conversation last night, she smiled as Calvin revealed he had missed her too. After that phone call, she had slept like a baby.

Looking up, she saw her Aunt Rowena on the porch, a phone in her hand and a notepad on her lap, writing furiously. Real estate signs were leaning against one of the columns next to the front steps. She was dressed in a long skirt, silk blouse, hose, flats and beautiful jewelry on her neck and ears. Closing the gate, she smiled affectionately at her aunt, the real estate mogul. They couldn't even sit on the couch in the living room because of all her client's folders perched there. She waved at her aunt and worked her way inside, stopping short when she realized her Aunt Genevieve was polishing the silver at the dining room table. "Well, if it's not our active niece. How was the walk?"

Grabbing a water from the fridge, Lillette plopped down in the chair in the corner of the dining room. A warning scowl appeared on her aunt's face, "Careful dear. If Ro caught you plunking down on her Chippendale chair, you'd be washing dishes morning, noon, and night."

Lillette snickered, but before she could say anything, her aunt's eyebrow rose and with a half-smile she said, "And yes, back in the day Chippendale had a different meaning. Hopefully, my niece is not one of those women who tuck dollar bills in the costumes of exotic male dancers."

She laughed and shook her head, "No, Aunt Ginny, but one of my girlfriends had a party and instead of watching movies and eating popcorn, we drank wine and watched men instead." Wrinkling her nose, she continued, "Of course, after about 10 minutes, I realized it really wasn't for me." She cleared her throat, "If I wanted to watch a man perform, I'd watch Calvin."

When Lillette ducked her head and her face turned red, her aunt stopped polishing an antique silver serving bowl and murmured, "Do tell. Your young man performs for you?" She grinned, "I never thought for one minute you had this side to you. I need some details young lady."

"Aunt Ginny, what am I going to do with you? It's not what you think." She gave a half laugh and explained, "I meant he's a gifted athlete and it's not a hardship at all to watch him work out. We run together and if it gets too hot, he takes his shirt off and…" she just shook her head and took a deep breath.

Her aunt put her hand on top of hers and asked, "And?"

Lillette reached over for a fan in the bowl on the counter behind her and began to fan herself, "Is it hot in here? I think we need to turn the air on."

Genevieve chuckled, "I think someone is very much in love."

Looking amused with her eyes sparkling she replied, "Oh, Aunt Ginny, I love him so much and he is one good looking man. He's got these crazy muscles and when he hugs me, his chest is so solid and I feel so safe with him."

"Well, young lady, good for you. Life is too short and you need to spend as much time with the ones you love. We all have careers and many things to do day-to-day but loving someone is the most important thing you can do with your life. I'm so glad." Her brows furrowed and she eyed her niece, "Now, I'm going to be frank with you. Not being married, you aren't making any decisions unbecoming to a young lady, are you?" Before her niece could speak, she held up her hand, "I know you are an adult and I'm not your mama, but I come from a different generation. I'm not saying all women of my generation waited for marriage, but with our family, it's the right thing to do. I'm not going to judge you, but I want you to have something special when you do make the choice to marry. You are worth waiting for because you are precious to us and we want the best for you."

Lillette rose from her chair and kissed her aunt on the cheek, "Aunt Genevieve, I love you and I will tell you that Calvin and I are right where we need to be in our relationship. I love him. We know what we want and that's all I can say."

Her aunt put her hand on her niece's cheek, "Well, as long as he's being a gentlemen and he's being respectful. We love you, Lillette."

She hugged her aunt, "I'm going to go take a shower, then I'll be ready for that lunch you two promised me at Pascal's Manale. It's been a while since I have visited you all and I need my BBQ shrimp fix. Thank you both for taking the day off." They glanced up to see Rowena through the window on the swing talking on the phone, then looked at each other and laughed.

Sated from their lunch, the trio exited the restaurant after spending a couple of hours eating and talking with several of the patrons and staff. Lillette had to smile as she followed her aunts to the car. Of course, her Aunt Rowena had seen several clients she had sold houses to and Aunt Genevieve ran into a group of women she volunteered with as an auxiliary member at the hospital. What surprised her the most was a framed photo of her Aunt Rowena with Harry Connick, Jr. hanging on the wall of the restaurant, riding a Mardi Gras float. Of course, her Aunt Genevieve rubbed shoulders with a famous Saints quarterback who had played for the team in the 1970's. She marveled at the picture hanging at the hospital she had visited last time of her aunt hugging the former Saints player at a charity event benefitting the hospital. Her aunts had a full life so far and she hoped they had many more days filled with rewarding work and special events.

Driving down St. Charles Avenue, her Aunt Rowena pulled over into a parking spot in front of what appeared to be a mansion with flags flying from the second-floor balcony and massive columns in the front. Lillette read the sign in front,

*Columns Hotel.* Turning around in her seat, Aunt Genevieve smiled, "Now, who's ready for a cocktail?"

Later that night, Lillette began to read a book she found on the shelf in her room. *A Confederacy of DUNCES by John Kennedy Toole* kept her entranced until the wee hours of the morning. She was awakened by her Aunt Genevieve, the book falling off the bed when she sat up, "Good morning, Aunt Genevieve." Stretching, she watched as her aunt picked the book off the floor, then looked over at the antique clock on the wall, "Oh my, 9:30? I really slept that late?"

Her aunt handed her the book as she sat on the bed, "Honey, you don't have a thing to feel bad about. After all, you're on vacation." Her eyes narrowed and her mouth turned down, "I guess that's the term people high up in Government call being fired."

Lillette sighed and put her hand on top of her aunt's, "I wasn't fired. It was actually decent of them to give me two weeks' paid vacation. Calvin said he went to bat for me as the evidence was circumstantial and they owed it to me since there was a leak somewhere high up and my name got into the news as a person of interest. He said he was just speculating, but he usually can ferret out secrets and details. He knows a lot of people in the city and he said they were obligated to make it right for me." She smiled and looked up to notice her aunt grinning at her, "What? Do I have something on my face?"

She patted her niece's cheek and answered, "Yes, the look of love for your young man."

She could feel her face redden as she put her hands on her cheek, "Well, I can't help it."

Her aunt replied as she winked at her, "I bet he can't either." Chuckling she nodded at the book her niece held, "How far did you get?"

"Almost done. I fell asleep. It's such an interesting book."

"Yes," her aunt responded, "Pulitzer Prize Winner. You should read the bio of the author. It's a very interesting story and that book is very popular." She patted Lillette's hand, "Now, since Rowena has gone to the office and I don't have to be at the hospital today, why don't we go out for some beignets and café au lait? And then we are going to meet your cousins later this evening for cocktails and dinner at *Irene's*."

She sighed, "You all are spoiling me. I love *Irene's*. Will the piano player be there tonight?" Lillette had fond memories of the last time she was at that restaurant.

"Yes, Marcus will be there. It's a special night."

She smiled, "So Aunt Ginny, you know the piano player? Must be a story to tell. Because last time I was there, an older distinguished man was playing and when I asked Cousin Lloyd about him, he told me he was a friend of yours." She raised an eyebrow at her aunt, "In fact, a VERY good friend of yours. What's that all about?" She watched as her aunt fussed around the room, straightening pictures and folding clothes on the chair by the bed.

"Oh, it's nothing dear." Clearly flustered, her aunt was pulling back the covers, "Now, out of bed, let's go. Hop to it. You must be starving."

Walking out of the room, she laughed and thought, "I'll find out tonight what that's all about." Lillette shook her head laughing as she headed into the bathroom.

# Chapter 12

*I*rene's was crowded when the aunts and Lillette were ushered in by Lloyd, a distant cousin she had only met a few times in the past. His two sisters had joined them, checking in with the maître d. Her cousin had insisted on driving the whole dinner party to the restaurant in his limo. He had retired from the corporate world and had partnered with a friend and opened up a limousine service. Lloyd catered to high powered clients, college parents who worried about their children's night life, and to Rowena. Lillette had to chuckle when her cousin told her that Rowena was adamant and told him as he was family, it shouldn't be a hardship to squire her and her real estate clients around town in a fine car. Plus, since businesses wanted to keep their customers and clientele happy, he was able to find parking in a town where that was nearly impossible.

Seated at a table, Lillette glanced around the restaurant. Candlelight cast a soft glow around the room. Missing Calvin, she looked across at her cousin and had to smile. She always thought of him as debonair. He had dark blonde hair which he parted on the side and a beard, which many men couldn't pull off, but he did. He was a very handsome man. His sisters were identical twins. Lucy and Lulu were turning heads all around the restaurant. Blonde and lithe, they seemed to take others' interests in their looks in stride. Lillette looked up when she heard a deep voice, "Well, good evening everyone." A man who looked to be in his late 60's stood by their table; his gaze centered on Aunt Genevieve.

Lloyd stood up and shook his hand, "Marcus, nice to see you. Music sounded great when we walked in. Can't wait for your next set."

The man moved his gaze from her aunt to Lillette, "Well, hello there. Whom do we have visiting us in our great city? Hmm?" Lillette took the man's hand he held out to her. He was a double for the actor Rip Torn.

Her cousin answered for her, "This lovely lady is our cousin, Lillette Baker from Mobile."

Marcus nodded in greeting, "I hope you've had a good time so far."

"Oh, yes. The aunts have taken me just about everywhere."

His gaze locked with Genevieve and he said, "I hope Genevieve took you to the Carousel Bar in the Hotel Monteleone. She always likes her cocktails." He winked at her aunt, "We've had some lovely visits there, haven't we Genevieve?" Lillette gazed at her aunt, who just nodded and displayed a strained smile on her face.

The visitor smiled, then offered, "I hope you enjoy your evening. Let me know if you have any requests. I do have a glass on the piano for just such a thing." He turned to Lillette, "Dear, the lamb and the chicken dishes here are superb. Have a good night."

They all turned to watch him go. A throat cleared at the table as Rowena said, "Well, Genevieve, he's as handsome as ever. So, we'll see you at breakfast in the morning?" She smirked at her sister, "Or maybe someone else will be treating you to breakfast."

Lillette watched in amusement as her Aunt Genevieve turned her head sharply and muttered something that sounded like, "Jesus Christ." All the cousins laughed and began to look at their menus.

Later that night, after a wonderful meal and great company, Lillette curled up in her bed and dialed his number. She heard the most beautiful sound. "Hello, my beautiful Lillette, how was your evening?" They talked for half an hour. When he heard her yawn through the phone, he chuckled, told her he missed her and that he loved her. Then he wished her a good night.

Two weeks flew by with Lillette caught up in the hustle and bustle of her aunts' lives. She worked with Genevieve one day at the hospital with her auxiliary work, tagged along while Rowena showed houses, and even went to run in City Park while the aunts sat on a bench and visited until she finished. She was walking off her run near the house early that last Saturday morning of her time in New Orleans when she spied a man getting out of a car that looked very familiar. A great big smile took over her face and she broke into a run until he caught her in his arms, "Oh, I can't believe you're here!" She held on to him tightly.

"Now, my beautiful Lillette, where else would I be?" he responded.

She looked over his shoulder, "And you brought Carla with you! I have missed you so much. What a surprise!" She put her lips to his and gave him a long kiss until she was breathless. Then she eyed him suspiciously, "Did the aunts know about this? Oh, I'm so going to let them have it if they did. They sure know how to keep a secret."

Calvin chuckled and replied, "Yes, it was all a covert operation to keep you in the dark so I could see that adoring look on your face when I showed up out of the blue." He released her and turned her around so she could see her aunts standing on the porch, their faces revealing that they were pleased as punch to see the new arrival.

Arm in arm, they walked up the steps to the porch. "Aunt Genevieve and Aunt Rowena, this is my Calvin. Isn't he great?"

Aunt Rowena was the first to respond, "Well, by the look on your face he sure is, and may I say he's a handsome devil too." She raised an eyebrow as her eyes warmed.

Aunt Genevieve added, "Oh, yes, I agree."

Calvin cleared his throat as he heard Lillette laugh, "Hey y'all, let's not embarrass the poor man after he drove all this way to see me." She turned to him and hugged him one more time, "Oh, I have missed you. Thank you for coming." Gently, she kissed his lips. As she turned, her aunts were beaming.

"Look how cute they are," said Rowena. She then clapped her hands, "Okay, children, let's go inside so we can talk about what we're going to do today." She grinned at her niece's boyfriend, "Young man, do we have plans for you."

As the aunts walked through their door, Calvin turned to the woman he loved, "Do I want to know?"

She raised her eyebrow, "Probably not. It's NOLA, baby. Just go with the flow." She laughed as he pulled her into his arms.

For the next two days, Lillette and Calvin helped Rowena with a renovation at one of her properties: a house around the corner from her own home. They carted out old boards, doors, and old appliances to be picked up the next morning by a local contractor. In return, Aunt Rowena set Calvin up in one of her properties near Magazine Street. When not helping the aunts, he and Lillette would explore the famous street to shop, eat and sip coffee at a well-known coffee shop. They were having a ball. The couple decided to stay for a few more days to help the aunts with anything they needed and to explore the city. Calvin escorted her to jazz clubs, restaurants and they even went to a gym to work out. Since her cousin Lloyd was a member, they were able to go there more than once. On their last night in the Big Easy, Lloyd drove the limousine and carried them all to a new restaurant called *The Holy Trinity*.

Calvin asked Lloyd how the restaurant got its name. He replied, "A young guy I'm friends with went through seminary and was going to become a Catholic priest. He got out before he made it official. Seems that he didn't like the decades of abuse that went on with children and decided to do something else instead because he wanted to help others. So, he finished a degree in counseling and now helps kids deal with abuse and the harshness of life. He still goes to church because he says he's not going to let what happened in the church ruin his faith in

God. He's a neat guy. His name is Charlie Weatherford. You'll meet him tonight. The best thing I like about Charlie is he hires people that have been through a rough time: the homeless, the abused, the forgotten…he helps them all." Lloyd looked over at Rowena, who was smiling. "Rowena, there, even helps Charlie by renting him some houses so he can give his employees a home. Some are small duplexes and some tiny houses, but they make do." He looked in the rear-view mirror only to see Rowena glaring at him, "What did I say that was wrong?"

Rowena replied, "I don't like to advertise what I do. That's not what that's all about."

"Come on Ro, believe me, Lillette and Calvin won't go putting that information in the Times-Picayune or all over Facebook. It's all good and it's a great thing you are doing." He laughed when he saw her expression. "Okay, everyone, let's go. I'm ready for some good Nawlins' food."

The group walked into the restaurant and were greeted by a man who looked to be in his 30's, bald, but with a serene countenance, "Lloyd, hey there. How are you?" The two men hugged and then Charlie looked at his companions, "Well, Lloyd, who'd you bring with you tonight?"

Lloyd replied, "These two ladies are sisters and my aunts. This is Rowena and Genevieve. Lillette is my cousin and this is her dear man, Calvin." Charlie gave everyone a hug as he welcomed the group.

The restaurant boasted an inside courtyard with a fountain in the middle. Charlie seated them at a lovely spot not far from the fountain. The hum of soft jazz could be heard throughout the restaurant. He passed everyone a menu, "We have anything and everything you could ever want. Oysters, po-boys and boudin are just a few of the things on the menu. Rachel will be here in a minute to take your drink order. Be right back with one of our appetizers." He smiled, "My treat."

A couple of minutes later a petite older woman with a cap of gray hair wearing a cross on a chain around her neck arrived at their table, "Hello, my name is Rachel. What may I get you all to drink?" Calvin, observant as ever, noticed that she had a couple of crooked fingers, which he'd bet his life had been broken. He also eyed a large scar under her arm when she wrote their drink orders down. Calvin averted his gaze as she looked at him next. He gave her his order and smiled. She gave him a beatific smile and gazed at him as if she could read his thoughts. She nodded and left to fill their drink order. He sighed when he thought of the abuse others went through on a daily basis. He had been called to many a home with his work in the police force and was glad when people got the help they needed. Calvin watched as Charlie made his way back to their table. It was a testament to kindness when others such as Charlie took in those who struggled.

Charlie set a couple of plates on the table and said, "We have fried green tomatoes with remoulade and Oysters Rockefeller." He glanced beside him as Rachel came to deliver the drinks, "Ah, Rachel, thank you very much." He looked back at the door, "Looks like I have more guests arriving. Please enjoy your appetizers. I'll be back to check on you all later."

The relatives and friends passed the time chatting and catching up with each other's lives as they enjoyed a combination of dishes for their lunch. Since both Mobile and New Orleans had finished with their Mardi Gras seasons, they all talked about the differences in the parades and floats in both big cities. As much as Calvin loved the happiness that time of year brought to everyone, he was glad the season had ended. With fun and merriment, he also saw his share of traffic violations, inebriated people, and massive crowds. He glanced to his right and captured Lillette's hand in his own. She looked at him and smiled. Calvin kissed her hand and then loosened his hold. When he looked up, her aunts were smiling. He winked at them and chuckled when he saw them grinning back at him.

The owner came back after their lunch and set a large king cake on the table, "We had a few in our freezer left over from Carnival and took them out this morning to share, on the house. Enjoy." As the family and friends dug into the wonderfully frosted cream cheese king cake decorated on top with purple, gold and green sugars, sighs could be heard around their table. It was the perfect end to a perfect New Orleans inspired meal. After thanking their host, the group made their way back to the shotgun house on State Street.

The next morning, after a breakfast of homemade beignets and chicory coffee, Lillette and Calvin were hugged by both the aunts with open invitations to visit again. Calvin opened the car door for Lillette, but she turned once more to see her aunts standing on the porch, waving to her. She smiled and blew them a kiss. The man she loved spoke up, "You ready, Love?" She touched his cheek and nodded. As he got behind the wheel, he waved once more to the aunts and moved Carla out into the street. As they rode through the city, Lillette put her hand on his and thanked him for coming to see her in New Orleans. He replied, "Oh, Hon, I think we will have a lifetime of adventures together. I can't wait to see where we will end up next." He glanced at her as he saw her smile. A few minutes later, Carla climbed up the ramp to the interstate and took the couple in love home.

# Chapter 13

The month of March in the city of Mobile brought in beautiful weather, the welcome budding of spring flowers, and marathons. The Azalea Trail Run began in the 1970's with hundreds of runners and built itself into a major spring event with now thousands of participants. Wally Sternum, his dad and Drew Myers met several friends one morning to be included in the race. Drew introduced the pair to Calvin and Lillette. Calvin asked about Georgia and the baby and Drew replied, "Oh, we are more than ready to meet the little one. Georgia is still working and we really like her new doctor that comes over the bay for appointments. She's got the room all ready." He looked over at Wally, "How's Adelia doing there, Dad?" He smiled when he caught the quick grin on Wally's face.

He answered, "The baby's just great. Leslie and I talked about bringing her out today, but we thought she was still a little too young to be out in such a big crowd." He smiled at his own father, "One day I hope she'll be running with us, right Dad?"

Wally, Sr. winked at him, "She'll probably beat both of us!" They all laughed.

Calvin looked at the group, "Hey, just want to let you all know that if we get separated, we have a tent for our government and law enforcement personnel. It's in Bienville Square. We have a group of officers that puts together refreshments and beverages for after the race. Everyone is welcome to meet back there."

Drew replied, "Thanks Calvin. Sounds good." As they heard the last call for participants to line up, the group was ready to go. Drew glanced over his shoulder and his eyes widened. About a dozen ladies, all dressed for the race, were waving at him. He smiled and waved back. He thought, "Why do they look so familiar?" He shook his head and turned around, ready to run. Soon the race began and the group took off. It was a great day for a run and by noon, many deemed the day a success. The group of friends were happy with the results and feasted on red beans and rice and a cold beer to round out the experience. Calvin and Lillette introduced them to several of their friends. They met Lillette's mom and Calvin's aunt, who was a counselor in the local school system. After giving their thanks for the food and for a fun day, Drew, Wally and his dad left to go back across the bay.

Since Wally drove, he dropped his fellow runners off at their respective homes and headed home to his family. He always felt like the luckiest man alive when he thought of the family he had created with Leslie. Wally thought he'd never love again after losing his first wife. Now, he was a husband and a father to a little girl and he would protect them with his life. Letting himself into their front door, he heard soft music playing and smiled. They usually played something soothing when trying to settle Adelia down. Leslie came to greet him in the living room with a kiss. He released her and said, "Hey, let me take a shower and clean up. Addy asleep?" He walked straight to the bathroom and took off his shirt. He grinned when Leslie leaned against the doorway and stared at his chest. He asked, "Like what you see?"

"Hmm, hmm, I sure do. You're still as lean and muscled since the day we married. As for our little girl, I sure hope she's asleep."

"Want me to check on her?" he asked, toeing off his shoes and taking off his socks.

"Well, that would be awkward, seeing that you only have your running shorts on and you'd have to jog to my parents' house to see her," she replied.

He paused in the act of taking off his shorts, "She's not here?"

Wally took a breath when his wife walked up to him and put her hands on his waist, "No, Mom insisted you and I have some time together. It's Adelia's first sleepover and I'm a little nervous." He didn't say anything, especially since his wife was helping him by sliding his shorts down. "But, I think, with your help, I can overcome my anxiousness." Her arms circled his neck and he put his arms around her waist. She continued, "What do you think?"

His lips met hers and then he said, "Well, I'm a little nervous too about not having our child in our house, but your parents did raise three children. I think they can handle it." He kissed her on top of her head, "I do appreciate their thoughtfulness." He gazed into her eyes, "You got clearance from the doctor, huh?"

She grinned, "Oh, yeah." She kissed him.

He took a breath, "So, we can pretty much do whatever we want, is that what you're saying?"

"And then some. We have all night," she replied. Leslie pulled back the shower curtain and pulled off her dress. She smiled as she watched her husband's expression when he realized she wasn't wearing anything else.

"Well," he said, "That's handy."

"Yeah, I thought so. I didn't think you'd mind me sharing your shower."

He looked at her and responded with a quick grin, "No ma'am, I don't mind at all." He gestured for her to go first, "I'll be right behind you."

With a glint in her eye, she replied, "That's what I'm counting on."

Laughing, he climbed into the shower behind his wife and with anticipation building, reached for the soap.

# Chapter 14

L illette had gone back to work with increased security in
the building at Calvin's insistence. He now made sure
that all government buildings had additional safety
measures in place for all employees and the public. The ongoing
case of who killed Noah Webster had yet to be solved. Calvin
had looked at every angle with additional detectives added to the
case to see if new evidence would turn up. He didn't want
Lillette to worry, so he hadn't shared his suspicions with her. He
had even met with Drew to get a fresh perspective. They had
both come to the same conclusion; that it was an inside job.
Now, Calvin just had to find out who would murder a city
employee and try to frame the woman he loved for the crime. It
wasn't as easy as it looked, especially when the general public
watched the crime dramas on TV and saw that crimes were
solved by the end of each show. That was Hollywood. This was
real life. Some crimes were never solved. He was going to push
hard until he could find out who killed Noah so he could get the
criminal off the street.

Each department had a lot to do to get ready for the
Solidarity Celebration. Lillette had much to accomplish and
wanted the freedom to do her job. She told Calvin she

understood where he was coming from and she wanted to be safe as well, but she was tired of always looking around her and waiting for the next shoe to drop. She wanted to get on with her life. Lillette told Calvin she would trust him to do his job as long as he trusted her to monitor her surroundings, in preparation for the big weekend in April. The Solidarity Weekend would mean a lot for the city and she wanted everything ready for the public to join in the fun and peaceful message. Calvin went with her in the evenings to Gavin's gym for boxing and self-defense lessons. She felt more prepared in defending herself. She practiced techniques and moves with Calvin over and over until he was satisfied that dealing with a threat had become second nature with her. Lillette finally felt secure in her backyard and in her home. It had taken a while and there were times she remembered the man who invaded her home for her car and her cash. She now carried her keys in her pocket and made sure her back door was locked when she cut the grass or worked in her backyard. Some people might think she was overreacting, but she didn't think so. She was safe once again and slept better at night.

Calvin installed an alarm system for her and told her it was an early Christmas present. She tried to argue with him that she should have bought the system herself, but he told her she could cook dinner for him one night and make his favorite dessert. She had hugged him as a thank you and he said that worked for him too. She smiled in remembrance. Lillette loved him so much. They'd both been so busy that the nights they were able to see one another was spent on the swing on her porch. He would put his arm around her and she would lay her head on his shoulder. Sometimes they would listen to music. Sometimes, they would bring out a bottle of wine to sip while on the swing.

And sometimes they would just sit in the quietness of the night. At the end of the evening, when it was time for him to go, he'd check her doors and windows to make sure they were secure for the night. Then he would leave her with a kiss and he'd tell her he loved her. She would do the same for him.

The Thursday night before the big weekend, when everything had been prepared as much as possible, Calvin texted her to let her know he'd like to pick her up for dinner. He felt like having seafood and asked her if she'd go with him. She texted him back with enthusiasm because she loved seafood. Carla made the journey to her house and carried them to a local favorite restaurant on the Causeway. With the tin roof and a wooden structure, the restaurant really did look like an old fishing camp. Calvin opened her door and held out his hand. She placed her hand in his and then he gently pulled her to him for a kiss. Lillette touched his cheek and said, "I love you, Calvin. I really do. I'm so glad to be with you."

He kissed her hand and kissed her once more, "Love, I know you do. I see it in your eyes every time we're together. I love you too." They held hands as they strolled up the walkway and into the restaurant. Seated by a window, they gazed at the stars and the moon in the sky overlooking the darkness of the bay. Calvin ordered a bottle of Merlot.

Sipping her wine, Lillette marveled at the view, "You know, I can only imagine how many alligators are in that water right outside this window." She turned her gaze to her date, "You ever go fishing in the delta?"

He shook his head, "No, can't say that I have. Friends of mine have fished there, but not me. I'm more inclined to fish off a dock, safe from all creatures that are under that water out there."

Lillette smiled, "When I was in college and home on a break, I had some friends talk me into taking an airboat ride at night." She blew out a breath and sipped her wine, "I've never seen so many beady eyes in all my life. It was scary, but also fascinating. Every time we ride over the Bayway, I hope to see an alligator." She laughed at Calvin's expression, "I couldn't tell you why, but ever since that time, I've been intrigued by them."

He shook his head, "My love, that's one thing we may have to compromise on. For some reason, I don't mind being in a boat on the Gulf, but I draw the line at being in a boat on the bay. I guess I've been on call for those accidents when a car or truck would go over the Bayway into the water below. We would interview the people who had to be rescued from the water and some were terrified by what they couldn't see under the water. I've never forgotten those stories."

She glanced at him, "Well, I can see where that would be scary. I had a friend who would always travel the causeway when she used to work in Mobile. She said she would be so grateful when she crossed all the bridges and finally made it to the road leading up the hill into the city of Spanish Fort on her way home. She couldn't shake the feeling that someday her car would blow a tire or someone would crash into her so she'd be stranded in the water. When she got married, she and her husband moved out of the area." Lillette smiled, "I still hear from her."

Calvin looked at her and asked, "So, she move into a suburb somewhere in the desert or in a busy city with no water surrounding her?"

Lillette eyed him and replied, "Pretty much. She now has two children and they do live in a gated community. Instead of swimming in a bay or the Gulf, they have a pool."

He smiled at her and sipped his wine, "Sounds like it worked out for her. Even though I may not like being in a boat on the bay, you still can't beat the view. In fact, I really like driving over the big bridge by the state docks. It's stunning. I had just turned 16 when I remember our parents driving over that bridge and seeing the tall ships that visited that summer. It was the best."

She smiled, "I was a young girl when they came through. I remember that. They were a sight to behold. That was the tricentennial year and there were many events going on from what I remember." She laughed in delight, "Oh gosh, we had a neighbor who had a baby that year and they had a day when they invited all the babies born that year into the Convention Center to take a picture. Then they sent all the parents a book with the picture. That was a fun summer."

Calvin grinned, "Was that when you realized you wanted to plan fun events for the city?"

She laughed, "No, not then. I was barely 10 years old and wanted to be a ballerina. My dream was to dance in the Nutcracker." She shook her head.

He put his hand on hers, "Well, did you?"

"No, I discovered my love of softball and that took care of that." She sipped her wine as the waiter came to take their order.

After the waiter left, Calvin asked, "So what is it you like most about Mobile?"

"Oh, Calvin, that's like asking me to pick out my favorite dessert or candy. I usually like them all." She looked at him, "I love going to all the museums, the different restaurants, the events at the Grounds and downtown. I just love this city." She took a breath and sipped from her glass of water, "What about you?"

He glanced out the window then back at Lillette, "I love to go to the high school and college games in the area: basketball, football, baseball…you name it. That's what I like."

As their food arrived, they ate, talked, and just enjoyed each other's company. At the end of the evening, Carla took them to Lillette's house. Calvin walked with her down the sidewalk and stood there while she unlocked her door. She turned to him, "Do you want to come in?"

He took her in his arms, "It's late and it's going to be a big weekend for us both. I might want to linger by kissing you for a while. I hate to keep you up if you need your rest."

She took him by the hand, "Why don't you let me worry about that. I've got some Old Dutch ice cream in the freezer and a DVD of Night Court. I know you like that show. What do you say?"

He leaned in for a kiss, "I say you had me at Old Dutch." They laughed as he followed her inside.

# Chapter 15

It was the first Friday in April when the 3-day Solidarity Celebration arrived. There were concerts stretching from one end by the majestic Cathedral to the famous center of Downtown that most locals just called the Square. The Chief of Police and his staff spent the better part of the afternoon helping close off streets and directing artists and vendors to their stations. When early evening arrived, the streets downtown were abuzz with people spilling out of bars, restaurants, and art galleries. Lillette felt like she had run a marathon setting up tents, lining up the musical acts, and handing out maps to those attending the Art Walk. Gavin found her, took the maps from her to hand out, while he made sure she ate the hot dog he provided and sipped from a bottle of water. She closed her eyes in ecstasy, savoring the best hot dog she had ever eaten. Her gaze roamed across the street to the owner of the hot dog stand that had been a mainstay in Downtown Mobile for as long as she could remember. Harry Dodge gave her a huge grin and a thumbs up. She gave him a smile and a thumbs up right back. She looked all around her and just took in the happy crowds and all the activities. Children and adults were having their faces painted, the library staff was handing out drawstring bags with pencils and small books for children and teenagers were dancing to the boy band in the square by the Cathedral. She just loved this city. She caught a glimpse of Calvin every so often. At those times, his eyes would meet hers, leaving no doubt for their feelings for one another. She took a breath and smiled. Glancing at her watch, she realized there was only 30 minutes left until it was time to close down the street festivities for the night. Saturday was a big family day throughout the city and then Sunday would be Worship Sunday Service at the Fairgrounds. Then worshipers and the general public were welcomed to participate in the Solidarity Walk that afternoon starting at the auditorium, crossing over a few main downtown streets, and ending at Mardi Gras Park.

Her thoughts were interrupted when Gavin took her hand and said, "Let's go."

"Uh, where are we going?" she asked as he led her down the street to Bienville Square. As they reached their destination, she watched as roller skaters circled the square for the Roll Mobile Friday night skate. The streets were closed off and an impromptu roller rink had been established for the public. There was a DJ that played hits such as *YMCA* and *the Hokey Pokey*. Many of the children and adults followed the dance steps.

A smile broke out on her face as she said, "Looks like everyone's having a great time. I'm so glad. I wish I had thought to bring my skates."

Gavin handed her a bag and said, "Your wish has been granted." He laughed and sat down on the curb to put on his skates. She looked dumbfounded so he tugged her hand so she was sitting next to him, "Come on, hurry up. We only have a half hour to join in the fun."

"How did you get my skates? They were way back in my closet."

"If you remember, I have a key to your house. While you were busy, I made myself at home. Those cookies you baked on the counter were great. Oh, by the way, you're out of Almond Milk." He looked at her and grinned, "Now, hurry up."

She looked down at the skates in her hand and said, "I don't know, Gavin, it's been a while since I skated." He looked at her in exasperation.

"Is there a problem here, Gavin? Is this young lady giving you a hard time?" Lillette looked up into the eyes of the man she had come to love. He was wearing a pair of roller skates. Behind him was her mother and several city council members, some detectives she had met and friends she knew from several of the area radio and news stations. Every one of them had on roller skates. The Chief of Police waved them on, "I have a situation here to remedy then I'll be joining everyone. Have fun and see you out there."

"Calvin, I haven't done this in a while and I'm just not sure..." He bent down and held his hands out for her skates. She handed them over. He took off her shoes and put on her skates. Making sure they were snug and secure; he then placed her shoes in her bag and put them in a skate bin. He stood up and held out his hand. "Calvin, I just don't know..." She didn't have another chance to say anything as he pulled her out to the street.

Gavin patted the chief's back and said, "Good job. She can be quite stubborn, but she's a good skater." He gazed at her and winked, "It will all come back to you. Now, if you excuse me, I have a date with an artist. See you later."

Lillette watched a petite young woman with auburn hair and green eyes wave to Gavin. She sported a pair of graffiti painted skates. He skated to her side and they took off around the curve in the street. "Huh," she thought, "I guess I'll get that story later." She looked up at Calvin and with her hand in his, began to move. She didn't want to admit it that her good friend had been right, but it was coming back to her. She glided forward and increased her speed slightly. She looked to her left and saw Calvin grinning at her, "Okay, so I'm having fun. Now, Chief, let's see what we can do together. I hope you're a strong skater."

He laughed, "Oh, just you wait. Here we go." He crossed his hands over hers and they skated together, scissoring their legs and moving to music such as *Thriller* and Motown classics. Lillette and Calvin moved into a dance position, hands on each other's shoulders and hips as they turned, glided, and moved as though this dance had been choreographed just for them. Their fellow skaters stopped to watch and the spectators clapped in time with the music. They just laughed and kept skating to the beat. When the music ended, they both took a bow when they heard cheers and whistles directed at them. Lillette was out of breath, but they took a few more laps around the Square to cool down and to enjoy the evening.

When the skating time ended, they exchanged skates for their shoes and began the process of helping shut down the festivities for the night. The vendors left, art galleries turned off their lights for the evening, and the Chief of Police made sure all police units had crowd control well in hand. Lillette and Calvin joined Gavin and his date for a late night dinner. They walked into a basement with an old bank vault which had been converted into a speakeasy, serving drinks and small plates of food. Gavin gave the password for the evening and a bookshelf slid back for entrance into the dining room. They were seated and ordered a round of drinks, listening to the smooth jazz of a musician playing the saxophone. Gavin made the introductions,

"Lillette and Calvin, this is Effie Baldwin. Effie, this is Lillette and Calvin. They work for the city and are friends of mine."

The Chief looked at Gavin and raised an eyebrow when Gavin mentioned him as being a friend. A smile appeared on Gavin's face. The auburn-haired artist spoke up, "Hello, I'm Effie. It's nice to meet you, Lillette. Gavin has told me all about his best friend's sister. All the events tonight were spectacular. Seems like you've had your hands full with your job."

She replied, "Yes, but I really enjoy what I do. Calvin is the Chief of Police for the city. He and his team have had to do a lot of crowd control in the city the last few months. Mardi Gras and several city events have kept us both pretty busy." She put her hand on his and he squeezed it. "So, Effie, tell me about your art. Seems Gavin has kept you all to himself. You are a very nice surprise, by the way." She wrinkled her nose as she watched Gavin glare at her.

Effie smiled at Gavin and then turned her attention to Lillette, "I'm a glassmith or you may have heard the term glassblower."

"Dale Chihuly," replied Calvin. Effie looked at him and nodded.

She answered, "Yes, exactly. I have been an admirer of his work for a long time. I've seen countless works of art with glassblowing, but I always come back to his style of art." She took a sip of her margarita and said, "I actually have toured the *Garden and Glass Exhibition* in Seattle. It's breathtaking."

Gavin nudged her shoulder, "Tell them how you got to Seattle. That's a really good story." He smiled and sipped his beer.

She smiled at him and bumped his shoulder, "Okay, since you're asking, I'll tell it." She glanced over at the couple seated across the table, "Gavin has a way of making me talk about my life when I'm actually a pretty shy person." Lillette raised an eyebrow at her friend and he smiled and shrugged. "Okay, let's see now. I'll have to start with telling you about my family. We moved here from Birmingham when I was little to help out my grandmother when my grandfather died. He was a veterinarian and would travel sometimes to Baldwin County to help a friend over there who was also a vet. Anyway, my grandmother happened to be a big art collector and she was a painter. She was very good too and taught me about the different mediums of art. So, when I was 18 and graduated from high school, my parents wanted me to go right into college. I wanted to be an artist and see the country first then eventually work my way to Paris. That was my plan.

My parents told me that was foolish and art would not be a good career for me. They wanted me to have a degree that would mean something." She shook her head and sipped her drink, "My grandmother went to bat for me and explained that I had worked hard and saved my money. She told them I had done everything they had asked of me. I had good grades all through school, had a great circle of friends and I never gave them a moment's trouble. We compromised. I got an Associate's degree in business management at a two-year college. My parents wanted me to then transfer to a major university. My grandmother wore them down for me. I had finished my two years and worked for another year. I went to Seattle the summer I turned 21. I ended up driving across the country with two of my girlfriends." She shook her head and sipped her drink.

Calvin said, "Sounds like a pretty straightforward adventure so far."

Gavin laughed, "Oh, just you wait. She hasn't gotten to the good parts yet." She grinned at him and just shook her head.

Smiling, Effie said, "Yes, our car made it as far as Mississippi. I was so excited about the trip that I forgot to fill the tank. Thank goodness I had an automobile service that came and filled up the car. So, after getting help with that, we stopped for the night in Arkansas. We found a little watering hole called the Rowdy Snake Pit."

Calvin laughed, "That sounds like a lawman's nightmare. Bouncers aplenty, huh?"

She laughed, "Yep. All kinds of interesting people in there. Pool tables, dart boards, karaoke, beer. Lots of young hot guys. What could go wrong?"

Gavin laughed, "Apparently, from what you told me, a lot!"

She continued, "Well, my friend Charlotte is a pool shark, so she won $200 off this one poor guy. Penelope is a dart fiend, so she won $100 off another guy."

Lillette took a sip of her water and spoke up, "So what was your talent? Did you bet anything?"

She grinned, "Well, Penelope bet me $20 that I wouldn't ride the mechanical bull they had in the corner of the room. So, I put a quarter in the juke box. They actually had a couple of songs from Urban Cowboy in there."

Lillette interrupted, "Urban Cowboy. The John Travolta movie?"

Effie nodded, put her hand on Gavin's and gazed into his eyes, "I did the Debra Winger slow dance she did on the bull. You know the one." She laughed and patted his back when he choked on his drink.

After he got his breath back he asked, "You did what?"

"Oh, you know that scene…" she began.

He took a breath, "Yes, I'm well aware of that scene of her on the mechanical bull." He took in her auburn hair, green eyes and petite frame. He bet she had been incredible. He cleared his throat, "There wouldn't be any videos around of that, would there?"

She laughed, "You'd be very disappointed."

"I don't know about that. I'm intrigued. I'd like to see you try that again sometime, but I don't think we have mechanical bulls in any of the bars around here, do we Lillette?" he smiled.

She laughed at her friend, "No, Gavin. Not that I remember." Calvin held her hand because it was so good to hear her laughter after what she'd been through.

Gavin propped his chin on his hand and looked dazzled by the woman at his side. Effie smiled and bumped his shoulder, "You are so gullible. I got on the bull and was thrown off immediately. Somebody had pushed the setting up to full speed. Thank goodness they had a mat around it that cushioned my fall." She shrugged her shoulders, "So instead of doing that, I took the cocktail napkins and charged $5 for caricatures. I sketched people who asked. It was all going well until this hot guy's girlfriend didn't like her picture I drew on the cocktail napkin. She had been rude all night to my girlfriends because her boyfriend was the pool player my friend beat. So, I guess her ill-mannered expression made it into her caricature because she got in my face to argue about it. Penelope and Charlotte came over to defend me and accidentally pushed her when they came to stand by the barstool. Then she shoved me, I fell off the stool and bumped my head on the bar." She took a drink from her glass and took a deep breath, "Then it was on. Penelope dumped her beer on the woman so that made her scream at her boyfriend to hit my friend. His expression was priceless. Charlotte grabbed our bags and pushed us out the door. We could still hear the girl screaming at her boyfriend. We ran laughing all the way to the car."

Calvin spoke up, "I hope you girls made it to where you needed to go after that. I'd hate to think you had any other adventures like that along the way." He looked at the lawyer in the group and smiled. Gavin was besotted and hanging on her every word.

She smiled, "We drove for another hour and spent the night at a motel off the interstate. We paid for it with some of our winnings from the bar. With three of us driving, we made it all the way to Denver the next night. We got there in time to go to a baseball game and ended up at a nicer bar than the one the night before. They had a great band. Thank goodness we found a cheap hotel. It took us a few more days to reach Seattle because we stopped along the way to savor the beauty of all the cities we drove through. We saw mountains, art and parks. Luckily, we had the foresight to bring a tent and sleeping bags, so we stayed at campgrounds along the way because they were a lot cheaper than hotels. We ate at diners or went to the grocery store and got sandwich fixings, snacks and fruit so we could eat in the car or outdoors. It was so much fun. Then when we finally did get to

Seattle, the art was incredible. We visited coffee shops, listened to bands and visited the Space Needle. We had a blast." She sipped her drink and took a deep breath.

Gavin spoke up, "And from all that, a glassblower is born."

"Yes, you could say that. I got an internship with a local glassmith and got permission to build a small studio behind the house I rent in Fairhope. It's an old farmhouse on land belonging to the Dalton family. They have a huge farm and their family is so nice. When the Future Farmers of America school groups come through, the students visit the studio and can watch me blow glass. We even let them take turns. Of course, they had to sign a safety clause first as part of their FFA paperwork."

"Sounds like you've got it going on," said the Chief.

She smiled, "I'm lucky. I have my pieces in several art galleries. I make an okay living, but I'm happy."

Lillette spoke up, "Can I ask you a question?" When Effie nodded, she continued, "How did you get your name? It's a nice name, but I don't come across it often."

She replied, "Remember that grandmother I was telling you about? My parents had no idea what to name me, so my grandmother came up with one. She really loved Paris but thought that name wouldn't define me. When I asked what she meant by that, she just said she could feel it in her bones that she had the right name for me. You see, she had lived in Paris when she was a young woman and walked by the Eiffel Tower every day. She thought it was the most beautiful structure and told me I was the most beautiful baby. So, Eiffel was shortened to Effie. I was really surprised that my parents went along with it, but my grandmother could be a formidable lady." She glanced at Lillette, "It seems I'm not the only one with an interesting name. Can I ask how you got yours?"

Lillette looked at Calvin then put her hand on her chest, "Me?" She chuckled, "I was told that mom wanted to name me Lilly and my father wanted to name me Paulette. So, it became Lillette." She smiled at Effie and added, "My name doesn't have the history yours does. That's a great story. Your grandmother sounds like a neat lady."

She laughed, "She's a pistol. She's still going strong at 80 and lives with my parents. And Lillette, I don't agree with you when it comes to your name.  It's a beautiful name," the artist replied.

Calvin said, "I agree." He reached for her, "Lillette and beauty go hand in hand."

She reached up and touched Calvin's face, "Thank you." He kissed her hand and winked at her. She smiled.

Gavin glanced at his watch, "Well, Effie, you ready for me to follow you home?"

"Now, I appreciate that, but I can't let you do that." She bumped his arm, "I've told you this many times and you don't listen, Gavin Jackson. You'd be going all the way across the bay and then having to drive back over here. That's too much driving for you."

"No ma'am, I'm a great driver. Just ask munchkin here, right Lillette? Remember some of those trips your brother, me and you had to the beach when we used to visit each other in college? Tell her that I'm a great driver. I never got any tickets." He glanced at Calvin.

"Oh my God! It's because when you got pulled over, you were lucky both were female officers and loved your curly hair and that dimple on your cheek. They let you go both times." She laughed and put her hand on Calvin's.

Gavin smiled, showing that dimple. "All right now, I got you where you and your brother needed to go, right?"

Lillette sighed and looked at his date, "Effie, all will be well. Let him play the gentleman and follow you home. He needs all the grace God can give him."

Gavin answered her back, "Ha, ha, ha. You're a riot, Lillette." He turned to his date, "Ready?" She nodded. They all said goodnight and two cars took off heading over the bay.

Calvin took his companion's hand and kissed it, "Ready for me to get you home? We have a big weekend ahead." She nodded, took his hand and they headed out.

# Chapter 16

Effie pulled up to the farmhouse. She turned off her car and grabbed her purse. By the time she closed the car door, Gavin was at her side. He walked her to the door and waited until she was inside, "Would you like to come in?" she asked, "That is, if you don't have to go home immediately."

He grinned at her and his eyes gleamed, "I got time. It would be nice to see your place since I haven't made it past the kitchen the times I've been here." Gavin had a tour of the farmhouse and even tried his hand at blowing glass in her studio. They ended up sitting in her kitchen, drinking coffee and talking. He glanced at his watch, "Wow, it's almost midnight. I didn't realize. I'm sorry, but I'm having such a good time." He stood and grabbed his jacket. She followed him to the door.

"Oh, wait a minute. Don't forget the vase you made." She smiled and handed it to him, "When we have more time, we'll get more intricate with colors, things like that."

He looked at her forest green eyes and leaned over to kiss her gently on the mouth. He eased back and gazed at her. He set the vase down on her table by the door and took her in his arms. As she was much shorter than him, her toes came off the porch as he lifted her up. He placed his lips on hers once more and deepened the kiss. Her hands held on to his back as she responded. He broke off the kiss and lowered her until her feet touched the ground.

"Wow, that was a really good kiss." She took a breath and stepped back.

He cleared his throat and replied, "Yes, yes it was." He grinned.

"There's that dimple again," she said smiling. If it was even more possible, his mouth opened even wider and he flashed his sparkling white teeth.

"I hope to see you again, Effie Baldwin. I had a very nice time on our date tonight."

"Oh, this was a date?" she smirked, "You've only been coming by the art gallery frequently for the last year and we've been going out for a while now. I feel like I see you all the time."

He looked down at the ground almost shyly, then lifted his head until his eyes met hers, "Yes ma'am, I do consider this a date. Why do you think I've been coming into the art gallery so much when you're downtown?"

"Because you like art?" she replied.

He shook his head, "Try again." He came closer to her.

She moved back a step, "You like to support the businesses in the Downtown area?"

She watched him move a step closer as he remarked, "That's not it, Paris."

"My name if Effie." She tried to step back and found herself with her back against the front door.

141

He took her hands in his and tugged her to him. He whispered, "You know why I come to the art gallery. Just like you know why I kissed you tonight." He lowered his head, "And it's the same reason why I'm going to do it again."

Her heart beat faster, "Oh, Gavin." She jumped up into his arms and his lips locked with hers, as he held on to her, kissing her like his life depended on it. When she could take a breath, in a teasing tone of voice she asked, "You like me, don't you? Red hair and all, huh?"

His mouth met hers once more and when he broke the kiss said, "Yes, all that wonderful auburn hair." He threaded his fingers through it. "You're beautiful, smart and talented. And you are so much fun to be around." He cleared his throat and he gazed into her eyes, "You know I love you."

 Her tone became serious and her eyes crawled to his, "I love you too." She touched his hair, "These curls are very sexy." She touched his face, "Since you showed me that dimple, that sealed the deal."

He laughed as he held her, "Did it now? Maybe one day I can show you more than just that dimple."

She smiled and thought, "Oh, I'm in trouble here." She took a deep breath, "Okay, lawyer man, I might take you up on that in the future. But, let's take our time and hold off on any other big adventure right now."

He thought he'd mess with her. He smiled inside, let her go and put his hand on his chest in protest, "What are you talking about? Oh, you thought I wanted something else. Wait a minute, when I said I could show you more, I meant my charm. What did you think I was talking about?"

She shook her head, "I'm not buying your act for one minute. You're a bright fella and you know what you meant." She put her arms around him and breathed in his masculine scent, "You smell so good." She looked up at him, "It's going to be so hard to keep my hands off you, but I'm made of stern stuff." She reached up to kiss his cheek, "Alright now, you need to go home. It's after midnight and you know nothing good happens after midnight."

He couldn't resist putting his hands on her cheeks and bending down to kiss her, "Oh, Paris, I beg to differ. There are many good things that happen after the clock strikes twelve." He touched her cheek once more and said, "Goodnight. I'll call you."

She replied, "That's a line if I ever heard one. But, since it's you, I'll be looking forward to it."

He stood by his car, "Now, I can't drive off until I know you are inside and locked up tight."

She grinned, "Got it." She made it to her door, turned and said, "Goodnight Perry Mason. Oh, and text me when you get home so I don't worry."

He grinned right back, "Goodnight Paris." He waited until she closed her door and he heard the lock engage. Gavin looked up at the sky and noticed how peaceful it was on the farm. The stars were out and the moon was full. He stared at her door again and thought about those kisses tonight. A goofy smile appeared on his face and he realized he couldn't wait to see her again. He got into his car and started the engine. Maybe it would be too soon to call her later today, "Nah, I'm totally calling her." He looked at his watch, "I guess I should wait until tomorrow night or even Sunday. Oh, hell with that!" Gavin picked up his phone and touched her contact number. It rang twice and then she picked up. He smiled, "Hi. I told you I'd call you."

She laughed, "Where are you?"

"I'm still sitting in front of your house. I just stopped to look at the stars, the moon, and thinking about the next time I can kiss you." He heard silence, "Effie? Hello?" He watched in disbelief as she darted out of her house wrapped up in a blanket. He leaned over to open her door. She climbed in, pink bunny slippers and all. He cleared his throat and smiled, "I like your slippers."

"Yeah, well, I like you." She scooted over and put her hands around his neck and pulled him in for a long kiss.

When he came up for air, he gazed at her pretty green eyes, "Well, this was totally unexpected. I figured I'd call you later and we could talk, plan our next official date." He touched a tendril of her hair, "But, I just couldn't wait."

She gazed right back at him, "We're in trouble, aren't we? This might be the fastest courtship known to man, huh?" He grinned at her and then he wasn't smiling any more. He plowed his hands through her hair and brought her lips to his. He kissed her with passion. She responded with abandon. They kissed for a few minutes more. He turned off the engine and opened the sun roof. Reclining their seats back, they cuddled together. Wrapped up in her grandmother's quilt, they watched the stars. Warm and content, they drifted off to sleep.

A rooster crowing had Gavin opening his eyes. His arms were around Effie. She had her head on his chest. He kissed the top of her head and she began to stir. Her eyes found his as she murmured, "Good morning."

"Good morning to you too, Paris. I had every intention of going home last night. Let me say one more time that this was totally unexpected, but very nice."

"Hmm. Yep. It seems like this is becoming a regular event, us falling asleep in your car, watching the stars. You know, I never thought I was the kind of girl to do something like this." A smile blossomed on her face.

"Believe me, Paris, I know what kind of girl you are. Why do you think I'm with you? You're lovely, inside and out." He looked at her, "All kidding aside, thank you for trusting me to be able to spend time with you like this. You know I wouldn't ever take advantage of you like that. I mean, I'd like to someday." Then he grinned, "Maybe after we're married, you'd cuddle up with me in my car to watch the stars again."

She snuggled closer to him, "Maybe after we're married, we'll just spread a blanket out in the backyard and just take it from there."

He took a deep breath, lifted her face with his hand and asked, "Paris, did we just propose to one another?"

She gazed at him, "Gavin, I feel like we have known each other forever. I'm so glad you finally asked me out. I've wanted to go out with you for a long time. You're a nice guy. You have a tremendous work ethic. You don't show it often when you come to the gallery, but you've visited me during your lunch break in your power suits and it's given me a glimpse of how you must be in a courtroom." She kissed him and looked at him once more, "Clarence Darrow, I bet you're an awesome lawyer. You're the real deal and the best man I know to trust my heart with." She touched his chest, "So, whatever we just agreed to, I'm in for the long haul."

He touched her face, "I appreciate the praise for my occupation. I made a pact with myself a long time ago. Basically, a lot of my clients come to me by word of mouth and my reputation. I grew up being honest and have heard a lot of jokes over the years about crooked attorneys and money grabbing lawyers. I like being different. I can handle myself and whatever comes along. I can see and smell bullshit a mile away and that's what makes me good at what I do."

She put her head back on his chest, "Gavin, about those three important words we say to each other. You know the ones I mean."

"How about breakfast? Those three words?" He chuckled.

"Well, we can definitely fix breakfast together. I've got some farm produce, fresh eggs, and good bacon. Mrs. Dalton just gave me two loaves of her bread she bakes. We can put together a couple of omelets with bacon and spinach. That sound good? Now, can we get back to our discussion before we got interrupted by you changing the subject? What about those three words?"

"We'll get to it." Teasing her, he kissed her and leaned over to open the car door. He asked her to open the front door to the house. Gavin swept her up in his arms and carried her inside. He kicked the door closed behind him and asked, "Which bedroom is yours again? I saw two upstairs on our tour."

Her breath caught in her chest as she gazed at him, "It's the one on the right, why?" Surely, he wasn't about to take her up there.

He abruptly put her down on her feet, shrugged and replied, "Just curious." Then a smile crept up on his face. It disappeared when she elbowed him in the stomach, "Oof. Oh my God, I hope I'm able to breathe again. What's the problem?" he asked as he rubbed his stomach.

"That was not very nice of you, since we just got engaged." She grimaced, "You know, I'm not one to take that next step with a man until I have a ring on my finger and a man says, 'I Do.' Just putting things out in the open here." She blew her red curls out of her face as she took the eggs and bacon out of the fridge.

He stepped up beside her and began cooking the bacon as she washed spinach and cracked eggs into a bowl. Gavin then asked, "So, you ever been married?" She looked at him and shook her head. He thought about that and with all the conversations they had this never came up. He took a deep breath and asked, "Paris, you mean you've never…with a man, ever?" He glanced at her and said nothing when she raised an eyebrow. He decided to change the subject, "I didn't know if you wanted to come over later and celebrate some of the city family day with us. I just have to run by my house, shower and change clothes." He held his breath and waited for her response.

She glanced at him and bumped his hip with hers since they were standing so close together, "Gavin, I know you're a good man. Why don't you tell me what's going on over in the city today and I can let you know?"

As they ate breakfast, he told her about the events for the day and the Solidarity Walk tomorrow, "Just let me know. I can always clean up the kitchen if you do want to come, give you time to get a shower." He cleared his throat because he was picturing her in the shower.

She grinned, "Get your mind out of the gutter. I see right through you. Lord, you are one red blooded male, aren't you?"

He grinned right back and leaned over to kiss her, "Can't help it. You're gorgeous, talented, and funny. It's a powerful combination for any man to resist."

She sipped her coffee and looked around her kitchen, "Okay, Gandhi, I'll take you up on that offer of cleaning up so I can grab a quick shower. I'm coming with you today."

He put his hand on hers, "I'm glad." He looked at her with affection, "You're very bright. Not many people know that Gandhi was a lawyer. You know, I do have a real name you could use." He smiled.

"Yes, and so do I," she smirked, ran her hands through his curls and jogged upstairs.

"God, I'm so done for," he laughed as he began to clear the table.

# Chapter 17

I t was a beautiful Saturday morning when Karen Dalton leaned out the window of the *Good to the Last Drop Coffee* food truck. As she handed over a cup of her finest blend to a customer, she felt a hand on her back. With no customers waiting, she turned around and hugged the man standing before her. "Well, Curtis, how do you think it's going?"

Her husband glanced behind her to make sure no one was standing there, then pulled his wife in closer for a kiss, "I think, Mrs. Dalton, that this food truck is a success. You've done really well and it's not even 10 A.M. yet." He took a breath, "I have to admit that bringing the truck to Mobile for the citywide family day was one of your best ideas yet."

She touched his cheek and watched his eyes darken with love, "I appreciate your support. It's wonderful having a partner to help me with the wholesale part of the coffee business and the food truck. The coffee shop still does a brisk business. I just hope this continues to be a success."

His arms loosened as he nodded towards the window, "Oh, I think that won't be a problem." He grinned as he turned her around to look at the line of teenagers jockeying up to the window. Since there was room for both of them at the window,

Curtis would took care of the payments, leaving Karen to make the coffee drinks. His wife's coffee was a hit. He was so proud of her. He glanced out at the sidewalk and saw more people getting in line. He was just glad that they carried a limited drink menu for the day. Looking at Karen, he smiled. She was in her element. Her job at the hospital kept her hopping during the week but starting the wholesale coffee business with her former boss brought her joy as well. She loved making her special blends and she told Curtis more than once that seeing people enjoy the liquid treats brought her much satisfaction.

After about 30 minutes, the line began to dissipate. She stretched her back, then briefly touched her stomach. She turned her head and met his gaze with joy and love. They hadn't told anyone yet, since they just discovered she was expecting. When talking about starting a family, they really had wanted to wait a couple of years, but Karen had gotten sick and an antibiotic had interfered with her monthly routine. So, when she felt something wasn't right, she went to see her doctor and had gotten quite a surprise. Karen made a special dinner that night and when her husband poured her a glass of wine, she had shaken her head and held out her hand to him. She asked him to sit down next to her and, as she explained what happened, his eyes had widened. He sipped her wine instead, then went to get her a glass of water.

As he set it on the table, he took her hand and kissed it. Then he tugged her close to him and smoothed her hair back. His mouth had met hers hungrily and they had retreated to their bedroom. Supper was eaten later that night. The next day, she received a bouquet of flowers. The card read, "I love you and can't wait for our next adventure." She smiled. It had been a special night. That was about three weeks ago and they still wanted to wait to share their good news with family and friends.

She told Curtis she would feel better about making an announcement in a few weeks as she wanted to make sure everything was fine with her pregnancy. He agreed. They stayed at the family day with the food truck until dusk. Then they closed up the truck and headed home.

On Sunday, Karen helped her mother-in-law with their church's annual spring festival. When she got home later that afternoon, she heard the shower running. She walked in and saw that the dining room table was set for supper. Candles were lit, their wedding china was placed on the table along with a package with her name on it. The words on the package jumped out at her, "Open me now please and follow the instructions on the inside." Smiling and shaking her head, she unwrapped her gift only to reveal a box. On top of the box, she read aloud, "Pull off the lid and follow the next set of directions." She grinned and, when she opened the box, nestled inside was the new Dalton Farms logo trucker's hat and she said, "Looks good." Karen smiled as she spied a note on the bottom of the box. She read aloud, "To my beautiful wife whom I love with all my heart. Meet me in our bedroom wearing this hat…and only this hat…see you there." Heart beating, Karen took off her shoes and socks, then unsnapped her jeans. Throwing her shirt on the chair, she made quick work of taking off her lingerie. Pulling the hat on over her head, she walked to her bedroom and stopped at the door. She grinned when she saw her husband sitting up in bed, a sheet pulled around his waist, with a matching Dalton trucker's cap on his head. Her eyes roamed over his muscled chest and up to his face. "Lord," she thought, "he is one fine looking man."

He smiled at her as he patted her side of the bed, "I like the hat." His gaze moved to her face, down to her still flat stomach and to her pink painted toenails. His blood heated and he could feel his heart race. As she came forward and put her knee on the bed, he took her hand and kissed it. His hand moved to rest on her stomach and love shone in his eyes, "Mrs. Dalton, I can't wait to see the changes to your body. I'm looking forward to it."

She leaned down and kissed him on his mouth, "Mr. Dalton, I love you." He pulled the sheet up and she scooted down to lie next to him. "Although, I think you're overdressed." He gave her an eye roll as he took the hat off and threw it on the chair across the room. She took her hat off and it joined his on the chair. Sighing she snuggled with her husband, her head lying on his chest, her hand caressing his shoulder. "Curtis, you smell so good." She turned and kissed his chest and felt his heart beating a little quicker. She grinned.

His hand caressed her arm as he breathed in the scent in her hair, "So do you." He placed his hand on her stomach, "You feeling okay?" He kissed the top of her head. Curtis smiled as he felt her nod her head.

She rolled over onto his chest and looked at him, "I've never felt better." She rained more kisses on his chest and then looked into his eyes, "and neither have you." With a wicked grin still on her face, her husband pulled her up his body and his mouth met hers.

Taking a ragged breath, Curtis remarked, "You're going to be the death of me." His eyes took in her flushed face and as his hands drifted down her back, he felt her move in just the right way to satisfy them both. With excitement building, he murmured, "But what a way to go." Their laughter filled the room. The couple touched and loved one another until they were sated with contentment.

Hunger for food drove them from their bed. Karen blew out the candles on the dining room table. Instead of the elaborate supper he had planned, Curtis made them peanut butter and jelly sandwiches. She threw on one of his button-down shirts and he was in his boxers, standing in their kitchen inhaling their make-shift dinner. He opened the drawer nearest him and pulled out an apron, "Want to put this on for old time's sake?" He grinned when he remembered the time he came into the kitchen to find his wife waiting for him, her body covered by an apron and nothing else. That had been a night to remember. He ran his hand down his face and couldn't keep from smiling.

Turning to the sink, Karen washed their dishes and put them in the drainer to dry. She turned to him and took the apron from his hand. His eyebrows shot up and she said, "No, I won't need this, will I?" She unbuttoned his shirt and let it drop to the floor.

He shook his head as she backed him up against the kitchen wall and he replied, "No, you won't need anything but me."

She pressed her body into his and nipped his ear with her mouth. Her hands wandered down his shoulders to his muscled chest and rested on his hips, touching the waistband of his boxers. "Do I need to help you with anything?"

He clasped his hands on her lower back as he exhaled a shaky breath and leaned against the wall, "Um, yeah, that'd be good." He gazed into her eyes as she undressed him. She was sweet, kind and all his. He didn't know how he'd gotten so lucky and so blessed. He wove his fingers through her hair and pulled her face up for a kiss. Curtis brushed his lips over hers gently then increased the pressure of his mouth. He savored their time together and showed her how much he loved her. Their breaths mingled and their bodies joined as one. They held each other tightly while their hearts finally calmed, at peace in the home they had made together.

# Chapter 18

The sun was shining and it was a beautiful April day for a Solidarity Walk. Yesterday was a great family day for the city. Everyone seemed to enjoy the activities and the businesses in the city thrived with the crowds.

Lillette took the elevator to Calvin's office. She was wearing a navy blue pantsuit and a pair of comfortable heels for walking. Her hair was pinned back in an elegant twist. She was so grateful that the investigation cleared her from any wrongdoing in the death of Noah Webster. There was still no clue about who killed him, but Calvin's department was being diligent in trying to get an answer. As the elevator opened, she stepped off and walked to the Police Chief's office. With a smile on her face and a radiant expression, she knocked and entered the room. Lillette took a deep breath, as he was the most handsome man she had ever seen. The love shining in his eyes for her amplified his attractiveness. He walked across the carpet to greet her. "Calvin, you are absolutely the best looking man in this whole building."

He stopped in front of her, put his hand on her cheek and lowered his mouth to the corner of hers. He kissed the other corner of her mouth. Then, his lips moved to hers and he pulled her into his chest. It was a kiss between two people who had come to love each other. He finally said, "You are one beautiful woman. You knew exactly what to wear to get our point across today."

She looked at his formal dress uniform with all the medals and his badge. Her hands brushed over his lapel, "My, I can't say it enough. You sure are handsome." She then glanced at her suit, "I thought I'd match you with the message of how important this walk is. We wear our best to show the citizens how we honor them. Then later, when we change for the Goodwill and Harmony Concert, we'll present a message of being together and making the city better for all." She walked over and looked out the window, "I hope the weather holds. The wind has already begun to pick up."

He walked to her and put his forehead on hers, "It will be just fine. Rain is not coming until later." He lifted his head and looked at her, "You make me so proud, Lillette. You understand me like no one else." He let her go and walked back to his desk, "I noticed you're wearing minimal jewelry for the walk."

She glanced at her ringless fingers and touched her small pearl earrings, "Yes, I thought understated would be best. Is there a problem?"

He came back around the desk holding a small blue velvet bag, "No, except for one thing." He knelt down in front of her and pulled the box out of the bag. He gazed at her and said, "Lillette, you have made me a better man. You have given me the strength and conviction to do my job and to lead a better life. I want to be with you. I want us to be a family. You, me and hopefully one day a child or two. I love you with all my heart

156

and would like to know if you would have me for your husband. You would make my life if you told me yes."

With her hand on her heart and tears running down her face, she nodded her head, "Yes, Calvin. I love you so much. I want to be with you and have a life and a family. I would love to have children to raise with you. It's all I've ever wanted." She felt the ring slide on her finger. It was a small sapphire surrounded by diamonds. "Oh, Calvin, I love you. It's a beautiful ring." She held his hand as he rose before her. She put her hand on his cheek, leaned forward, her mouth lingering on his. He held her close and moved his mouth fervently over hers. He then pulled her in for a hug and hung on tight. They heard a knock on the door and his secretary said, "Five minutes, Chief."

He cleared his throat and called out, "I'll be right there." He looked back at the woman he loved. He never thought this day would come. He moved his hands down her arms, "We're walking together, hand in hand, you, and me. Not just for today, but for the rest of our lives." He kissed her forehead as moisture formed in his eyes. He gazed at her and asked, "Are you ready to go, my love?"

She wiped her eyes and kissed him once more, "Yes, I'm ready Calvin. I'm ready to begin our life together." The Chief of Police and the Events Coordinator walked hand and hand out of the Government Complex and onto the sidewalk. Lillette looked around at all the people waiting to follow Calvin. Her mother stepped up to the front line next to her daughter. Lillette discreetly showed her mother the ring. Her mom hugged her and they smiled at each other. Calvin caught her mom's smile and he winked at the councilwoman. Other city council members stepped up next to her mother. Many city officials, business owners, religious leaders, and families gathered together clasping hands. Holding his hand, Lillette walked next to Calvin. Many of the citizens joined them. People were parking their cars and getting in line with the crowd gathered to show solidarity.

Police officers were stationed at the corner of several main intersections as the citizens all walked to Mardi Gras Park. Many tents and tables had been set up with information detailing city events and agencies to help the public. There were medical teams to inform people about healthcare and much more information to provide for the needs of the residents of the city. As they reached the park, Calvin held on to Lillette's hand. Gavin and Effie stepped up to hug her and admired her ring. Gavin grinned and leaned over to shake the hand of the Chief of Police. They all looked around and were amazed at the turn out. The vendor booths were stacked with people taking pamphlets and talking to the professionals that volunteered their time today. Many came up to Calvin to shake his hand or ask him questions. His fiancé squeezed his hand and told him she was going to visit the booths with her mother. Gavin and Effie moved away to walk in the other direction towards the tents with displays of art. Lillette looked back one more time and caught the eye of the man she loved. He winked at her and smiled. She blew him a kiss. She smoothed down her hair as a gust of wind blew through the park. The vendors were grabbing brochures and she helped by storing them in the boxes provided. She crossed her fingers when she looked up at the gray clouds in the distance.

Calvin talked to children and their parents, business leaders and met many people he did not know. He was concerned about the weather as the wind began to whip up around the area. The wind downtown could be fierce once it started. Calvin was happy. He was going to be a married man and the solidarity walk was a success. So far, so good. Everyone was well behaved. The mayor stepped up next to him and said, "Nice job, Calvin. Looks like a great day for the city. Do you mind giving me a minute in private?" The Police Chief nodded and followed the mayor down the sidewalk away from the crowds until they were standing in the deserted fort across the street from the park. He turned to the mayor who said, "Listen, I appreciate your assistance with trying to find out who killed Noah. I'm glad Lillette was cleared. I came across something I thought you should see." The mayor pulled out an envelope from his inside suit pocket and before he could hand it to Calvin, his phone began to ring, "Sorry. It's my wife trying to catch up with me. She's going to meet me at the park before it rains so we can go home together. Don't go anywhere. I'll just be a minute." The mayor jogged across the street.

Calvin walked to the entrance to the fort. He spotted the woman he loved at a booth and smiled as she talked animatedly with a local author who he recognized as a writer from across the bay. From what he remembered this particular woman was working on a series of romances with local settings. Lillette turned and looked across the street and saw her fiancé. She waved at him and he waved back. Saying her goodbyes to the woman, she stepped to the sidewalk to cross the street when she heard Gavin call her name. She smiled as he and Effie approached. They had their heads together as she was admiring the painting the artist was holding. Lillette looked back one more time at Calvin and smiled. He grinned and then her attention turned back to the painting. She heard someone yell, "Hey Chief!" Then she heard three shots in quick succession.

People ran as Gavin pushed her and Effie to the ground and covered them as best he could. Officers were yelling and getting everyone to safety. Lillette tried to get up, "God, no! Calvin!" She was frantic, "Gavin, let me up, let me up!"

"Stay down." Gavin looked up as officers were running across the street to the fort. He saw a doctor he knew kneeling over a man dressed in blue at the entrance to the fort, "Oh, no." As he released his hold on Lillette, she scrambled up and ran across the street. Two officers held her back and she screamed and tried to break free.

She cried his name as she choked on her tears, "Calvin!" She yelled at the officers and tried to squirm from their grasp, "Let me go!" Her mother hurried to her daughter and told them to let her go. As she was released, she ran through the officers to get to Calvin. She got her first glimpse of him and fell to her knees as blood gushed out of his side and from his shoulder, "Calvin, come on love, stay with me." She held his hand as the doctor worked trying to stop the bleeding. She heard sirens as an ambulance pulled up to the fort. She saw her fiancé open his eyes and she tried to reassure him, "Calvin, that's it. You're going to be fine." Tears streamed down her face, "Come on baby, hang in there with me. We're going to have such a good life. Please, Honey."

She felt him squeeze her hand as he gasped her name, "Lillette. Love you. Live a good life. I'm sorry. Remember always that I love you. Thank you for loving me. Wish we had time. You are…so special. Find someone to love and don't let go." He tried to take a breath, "Love…." He stopped talking and his head lulled to the side. She watched as the doctor and the EMT's got into the ambulance and began chest compressions.

She responded as she choked back a sob, "I'll be right behind you. Before you know it we'll be married and spending the rest of our lives together." She heard them say what hospital they were taking him to as the doors closed and the ambulance sped away. She turned as her mother tried to hurry her to the car through the crowd. They became separated as she shouted for her mom, crying, and panicking in her need to get to Calvin. She heard someone call her name. She looked up and saw the Assistant Chief of Police rushing to get to her, "Mack, I got separated from my mother. I need to get to the hospital. Please."

He put his arm around her, "Yes, dear, come with me." She heard someone calling her name. She whipped her head around but couldn't tell who it was. Then she heard it again. She couldn't see over the crowds and Mack had tightened his hold to move her through the crowd. "My car is just over here." He walked her to a spot by the hotel across the street and motioned for her to get into the front seat of a long black limousine after opening her door. She finally looked at him and noticed him sweating. His face was red.

"Mack, are you okay?" she asked, "And why are you driving the limo today?" She reached in her pocket as her phone began to ring. It was her mother. She answered and told her mother she got a ride to the hospital and would meet her there. She hung up and noticed her companion putting a bag on the seat beside her. It had fallen open. Lillette got distracted when her phone rang again. It was Gavin. She looked up and saw him coming through the crowd. Mack was opening the door to the back. The partition was up. Then she heard the trunk open. She was anxious to get to the hospital. An envelope had fallen out of his bag and it had Calvin's name on it. She picked it up and slipped the contents out, "Oh, my God." In her haste to get out of the car, the papers spilled to the floor. Her door wouldn't open.

Her companion joined her and saw the papers scattered on the floor. He looked at her and noticed the tracks of tears on her face and the horror in her eyes. "Well, now you know. But it won't do you any good. There's no way out. I had to do it. The Chief and the mayor were on to me. Noah was a sanctimonious ass. He was in on it with me. Noah owed some money to some very unsavory characters. He was the one that mowed down Calvin in that car across the bay. He wanted to try again and I told him to wait. He was too impatient and threatened me. I sacrificed everything for this job. My wife left me. My daughter wants nothing to do with me. I needed the money. I just need a little more time to hit those numbers at the casino. It's my time. I'm going to win a lot of money."

She was terrified, "This was all about money? You killed Noah and you shot Calvin. All because of your gambling addiction, you stole money that was supposed to go to the homeless program, the shelters, and the advocacy centers for children. Oh my God, what kind of a monster are you?" She was trying to buy time but needed to get to the man she loved, so she tried reasoning with him, "Please, I need to get to the hospital. Just let me out and you can leave. I just want to see Calvin." She tried the door again.

He laughed and then looked at her, his face reddening as he grabbed her arm, "You won't leave it alone. I have to deal with you. I'm sorry dear. You did so much for the city. It's a shame you killed yourself out of grief once you learned Calvin was dead. He's gone Lillette. Those shots I fired were right where they needed to be. I guess you don't remember my many awards as a sharp shooter. All it took was finding a spot on the building across the street and the rest, as they say, is history."

She had to stay calm for the man she loved, "No, he's a fighter. You have no idea."

"It's okay, I'll make sure when I put a bullet in you that it will be quick." He started the engine and took off down Royal Street, the sound of the wind beating against the car. Rain began to lash the windshield. She saw Gavin finally break through from the crowd as she began to bang on the car window to get his attention. He began running towards the car with Effie running behind him. Tears were clouding her eyes and she wiped them away. She had to be strong. She would know if Calvin was dead. All of a sudden she heard banging on the partition and then it shattered. She looked back and saw the mayor laying on his back, his feet in the air. He had worked his way up to the divider and had kicked out the window. As the car sped up, she had to act. She tried to grab the wheel and Mack shoved her off, hitting her head on the car window. She wasn't going to die today. She grabbed it again. The car veered to the left, then spun around and stopped in the middle of the street, causing Mack to hit his head on the steering wheel. Blood oozed out of his head and he looked disoriented.

This was her chance. She reached over and hit a button. The sun roof opened. She cried out and tried another button. It clicked and the locks were released. Gavin reached the door and held it open, the wind blowing mightily in its fury. He grabbed Lillette. He heard Effie behind him say, "Gavin, hurry! Oh my God!" He turned around with Lillette in his arms and saw Effie looking up at the top of the building next to them.

He backed up and followed her gaze, "Oh, no! It can't be."

Fighting the wind to get the back door open, Lillette watched in horror as the electronic Moon Pie used for the New Year's Eve Moon Pie Drop, suspended on top of the bank building, swayed in the wind and broke out of its hold and began to descend at a breathtaking clip. She yelled, "Hurry! We have to get the mayor out! Help me get the door open!" It took Gavin holding the door and the two ladies lifting the mayor and scooting him out. They all backed up and looked as the 600-pound moon pie bounced on the edge of the building six stories above them all. They began to run across the street to the hotel. They turned as they heard yelling coming from the limousine.

The Assistant Chief of Police had moved and had raised himself up out of the sunroof, blood dripping from his head and he was pointing a gun at Lillette, "You thought you'd get away. You and your boyfriend are the cause of all my trouble. You're done." He aimed the gun as they all hit the ground. Mack saw a group of police officers begin to run down the street. They'd never make it before he took her and then the mayor out. He heard yelling. The Assistant Police Chief smiled and stretched his arms out, feeling powerful with the wind and rain surrounding him. Nothing could stop him now. He took a second to look up at the sky and never even got the chance to yell as the electronic pastry crushed him and split the body of the car in half. The force was so strong that the street cracked below the car. One of the police officers ran to the mayor and used a key to uncuff him.

Lillette shuddered and turned away. She saw her mother's car come barreling down the side of the street. She saw the officers begin to react and she shouted, "No, that's Councilwoman Baker. Don't hurt her!"

The car stopped and everyone got in, except for the mayor who said, "You all go to Calvin please. I'll take care of things here." He waved them past a car parked near the hotel. Lillette's mother peeled off down the street. Many people now surrounded the car crushed by the giant Moon Pie. The mayor gave orders to his city crew, "Okay, let's get some orange cones up. We have a crack in the street and we need to get this mess cordoned off so no one gets hurt." He looked up and saw a few detectives walk up to him, "It's a crime scene so start processing and then we can take it from there." The mayor put his hands on his hips, looked up at the top of the bank building and shook his head. He looked to his left as the city councilman responsible for getting the Moon Pie for the city came to stand beside him. They both stared as the city workers and police officers scrambled to do their jobs. The mayor sighed, "Yes, I know." Even with the harshness of the scene before him, a little humor escaped the mayor's lips as he spoke up, "Sure you don't want to replace it with another symbol like a replica of the USS Alabama, a large shrimp or an oversized azalea?" The leader of the city could feel the weight of the stare from the man standing beside him. He let out a breath and put a hand on the councilman's shoulder, "Okay, I'll start working on getting another Moon Pie." The mayor turned, grimaced at the scene before him and joined his crew.

# Chapter 19

L illette paced in the waiting room at the hospital. Calvin had been in surgery for a couple of hours now. There was nothing she could do but mark time until they had an update. Her mom put a cup of coffee in her hand, "Mom, I don't want anything, please."

Her mom gave her that look that only moms around the world could get away with, pointed to the coffee cup and said, "You'll drink that." She handed her a protein bar, "And you'll eat this." She smoothed her daughter's hair and softened her tone, "You won't do him any good if you don't take care of yourself."

Her eyes watered and she managed to say, "Thank you." Her mom led her to a seat next to Gavin and Effie. Her friend winked at her as he put his arm around the artist he was seeing. She was glad for them. Her thought was she'd never put them together as a couple, but seeing them now, she got it. There was a silent communication between the two; a glance, the way she rubbed her hand on his arm, and the smiles they shared when they thought no one else was looking. Lillette sighed, ate the protein bar and drank her coffee.

A couple of hours later, she paced the lobby, waiting for any word. She looked across the room and saw that Gavin was holding Effie, who had fallen asleep. Her mom was drinking a cup of coffee, looking out the window at the parking deck below. Then, movement came from the double doors down the hall. She watched as a doctor walked towards them. He looked tired and had the best poker face she'd ever seen. Lillette couldn't tell if the man she loved was alive or dead if the doctor's expression was anything to go by. She held her breath as he got closer. With his hands on his hips, he nodded and asked, "Are you the family of the Chief?"

Gavin roused Effie as they both stood, Lillette's mother coming to stand by her, placing her hand on her shoulder. Her mother answered for her, "Yes, we are his family. We have been waiting to hear. How is he?"

The doctor shook his head and Lillette's heart sank. She grabbed her mother's hand as he spoke, "He's unconscious, but stable. I'm going to be honest with you. The next twelve hours will be crucial for his survival. From what I can tell, it helps that he's in great physical condition, but he lost a lot of blood. We hope for the best." He ran his hand over his head, "You might want to go home and get some rest. It's going to be a long night. We have your contact numbers. The nurse will call you."

The doctor turned to go when Lillette put a hand on his arm, "Doctor, is there any place I can stay to be close to him? You see, we just got engaged today and I want to be near him. Please."

He began to shake his head, saw the tears in her eyes and sighed, "It's highly irregular, but not unheard of for family members to stay the night. Many times, I have seen people stay out here in the lobby for the evening, but there is another option." He led them to a small waiting area closer to the Intensive Care Unit. "There are certain times when you are allowed back in ICU to visit with him, but you can't stay there overnight. You can remain in this waiting area. The door closes and there is a couch there if you'd like."

She nodded her head and looked at Gavin, Effie and her mom. "If you all want to go home, I'll wait here. I just can't leave. I need to be here with him." They all gave her a hug and she promised to keep in touch.

Her mom spoke up, "I'll bring you some coffee and breakfast in the morning and a change of clothes. Okay?" She hugged her mom and watched as she walked out with Gavin and Effie. She moved to the waiting room and shut the door. She noticed someone had brought her a pillow, a blanket, a pack of crackers and a bottle of water. She noticed a small TV mounted on the wall and a table full of magazines. She flipped through a magazine and got up to pace. Being keyed up and worried about Calvin kept her from lying down to rest. Lillette opened the door and walked down the hallway and then back to the room. Reading a book for a while, her head began to fall to her chest. Finally, laying her head on the pillow provided and pulling the blanket over her, she slept.

Lillette woke as she heard a voice say her name. She looked up and it was the doctor from the night before. She sat up quickly, holding her breath. She released it when she saw a smile on his face. "Young lady, your fiancé is awake if you would like to see him." He grinned when she scrambled up from the couch and slipped into her shoes. Following the doctor, she walked into the ICU. He led her to a partitioned room and there he was. Her feeling of relief quickly turned to a flood of tears running down her face. She moved closer to the bed and then heard the closing of the curtain behind her. The doctor had given her privacy to see her beloved.

Calvin's eyes were staring at her. She realized he was still very much out of it. Lillette didn't care as she put her hand on his, "Calvin Wynfrey, you gave me a real fright. We're done with anything else happening to you, do you hear me?" She bent down and kissed his mouth. He closed his eyes. She took a deep breath, "I love you so much." Spying a chair in the corner, she moved it closer to the bed and just held his hand. Looking at the monitors, she sighed and was so glad he was still with her. Life without him would be unthinkable. They allowed her to stay for another half hour, then told her he needed to rest. She put her hand in his and squeezed. She turned to move her hand and felt a small tug. A grin broke out on her face as she realized he was trying to squeeze her hand. Lillette kissed his cheek, "I love you. I'm right around the corner in the waiting room. I'm not leaving you. I'll see you soon. Get some rest." She walked to the curtain and pulled it open. Looking back one more time, she blew him a kiss and smiled.

A few weeks later, Georgia and Drew Myers welcomed their son into the world. Sidney Andrew Myers was born during the middle of the week at the end of April. It had been a blustery and rainy day. Inside the hospital, the family was cozy and the baby warm and safe in their private room. He was being held in his mother's arms. Drew and the mamas were passing around a box of tissues due to the tears of joy in the room. Drew leaned down, kissed his wife, and wiped his eyes, "He's just perfect."

He gently laid his hand on the baby's foot. Sidney kicked out and he laughed, "Well, we either have the makings of a sports star or a really good detective who can kick some serious…" He was interrupted by his wife putting her hand on his mouth.

"Not in front of the baby, Dad," Georgia remarked. He kissed her hand then once more leaned down to his wife and his lips met hers. She rested her hand on his cheek and gazed into his eyes, "I love you."

He grinned, "I love you too, Cherie." The newest addition to the family was held and fussed over by his grandmothers. After visiting with their grandson, the mamas kissed the young couple and said their goodbyes. With Georgia drifting off to sleep, Drew sat in the recliner near the window and held little Sidney. He took off the baby's cap and smoothed his hand gently over his son's head, "Oh, you are a fine one, Sidney Andrew Myers." He looked up to heaven, "Thank you for him. I assure you that I won't let him down." He gazed at his sleeping wife with love, "Thank you for her too. It's a hell of a thing to think about that something as awful as her losing you and her battle with Calvin brought me into their world." He looked down at the tiny bundle asleep in his hands, "Okay, little man, I'm going to let you rest." Drew put his son into the bassinet provided by the hospital and wheeled it next to Georgia's bed. He picked up his water bottle, drinking thirstily, staring out the hospital window. Drew looked up as the hospital door opened and saw the doctor as he came into the room. He shook his hand, "Hey, Doc."

Spencer Hawkins came over to look at little Sidney, "Hey, little man." He picked him up and looked him over. "You sure are a cool little dude, aren't you? You are one fine baby boy." At that moment, Sidney decided to make his presence known with a lusty cry. "Yeah, little man, you tell us how you feel." Spencer glanced over at the bed, "Well, hello Mom. I think someone is hungry." He walked to the bed as Drew moved to the other side to help Georgia sit up. "Okay, young man, time for dinner." He handed the baby to Georgia and said, "I'll let you have your privacy. Just wanted to make sure you were you're feeling okay? You did a great job."

She clasped his hand, "You too, Spencer. I'm feeling very well." She touched her baby's cheek and just grinned. She looked at her doctor and said, "Thank you so very much." The doctor winked at Georgia, patted Drew on the shoulder and pulled the door closed.

# Chapter 20

Spencer turned in the hallway outside the room and got quite a surprise. Leaning against the nurse's station was Sadie Monroe. She had her jacket in her hand and almost looked like she was waiting for him, but that couldn't be. They were like oil and water. She wouldn't willingly be here for him. He usually was a grumpy bastard when she was around. He couldn't help it. She was a beautiful and kind woman, although around him she didn't mince words about his own medical care and what she thought he should do when working overtime. Well, she should know that babies don't care what time it is or how much sleep you've had. But he freaking loved his work and wouldn't have it any other way. Putting his hands in his pockets, he strolled over to her, "Well, Sadie, still hanging around? No hot date tonight?" As soon as the words came out of his mouth and he saw her hurt expression, he felt like an ass.

Sadie looked at the doctor she had feelings for, but of course, she never tipped her hand or told him how she felt. There was no getting close to him. He had a wall up that was ten feet high and he didn't let anyone into his life. She knew all about his father cheating on his mother and how he felt about his father. She only found this out because she happened to be leaving the building where they both worked one night when his father came to have a talk with him. She stuck around because she heard yelling and wanted to help Spencer if it came to that. She overheard Spencer yelling at his father to get out of his office, that he wanted nothing to do with a man who would cheat on his wife. Spencer was getting more upset by the minute and his father wouldn't leave. She took a deep breath and waited by the door to his office. She spoke up, told him there was an emergency and they had to go. His father looked at his son and ignored her. Sadie smiled inside because she had grown up with a father that was as much a bastard as Spencer's. When his dad left, she locked the outer door to the building and when she turned around, Spencer was there with his bag. When she explained why she had lied about the emergency and that she was just trying to help, Spencer stared at her and told her to mind her own business. He waited until she got into her car and then he got into his own car and pulled out of the parking lot. As far as she knew, his father never visited him again.

Looking at Spencer, she sighed and said, "I was just checking on Georgia. I knew she was here over the bay and figured you'd be here too. You know Georgia and I have kept in touch ever since she had the fall in her home that time and she was worried about the baby. I understand she had a little boy." She saw the look on his face and decided to leave, "Yeah, I'll just come back. If you'll tell me what time you'll be checking on her tomorrow, I can come when you won't be here. That way, you won't have to make degrading remarks to me and I won't have to hear them or see you." She turned to leave when she felt a hand on her arm. He guided her to a corner away from the nurse's station.

"Sadie, listen." He ran his hand through his hair and muttered a curse word, "I didn't mean that like it sounded. I'm just being my usual asinine self and you should know better by now not to listen to anything I say. I'd hate for you to have to drive all the way over here tomorrow when you're here now." He took a breath and shifted, "Listen, she's feeding the baby." He looked at his watch. "I happen to have a few minutes and I'm about to rock your existence as you know it, but here goes." He gazed at her beautiful blue eyes and asked, "Why don't we go to the cafeteria and have coffee while she feeds Sidney?"

She looked back at him, smiled, and replied, "She did name him after her late husband after all. I was wondering."

He said, "Well, Sidney is his first name from her late husband and the middle name is Andrew in honor of Drew. So, coffee?"

Sadie looked down at her feet, then glanced back up at Spencer. She remarked, "Well, I guess after you've been such a jerk, it would be only fair for you to buy me a cup of coffee."

She was so surprised when he grinned and she watched in amazement as those warm brown eyes of his crinkled, "Nicely put, Sadie." He gestured for her to go first since the hallway was getting crowded with visitors and medical personnel checking on patients. Once they got their coffee in the cafeteria and settled at a table, he cleared his throat and said, "You must be really busy upstairs in our building, because I don't see you as often." He didn't even want to admit to himself that seeing her brightened his day, at least for a little while. He would like to get to know her better, but he didn't want to ruin her life. The few relationships he had in the past didn't amount to much, except for one. Spencer shook his head. He pretty much cared for himself with no problem at all, but a prosthetic leg had put a few women off. The last time he tried to get close to someone, the woman he was with got turned off after he slept with her. She had pitied him because of his leg and she just wasn't comfortable being with him. It hadn't helped him at all when he had a nightmare about losing his leg and it had left her shaken. It would have been a lot for anyone to deal with. She was a lovely woman he had gone to high school with and they were reconnecting when she came through to visit her family. She had apologized for being so shallow, but she had always been nice to him. He couldn't blame her. His long hours didn't help, but he had always wanted to be a doctor and couldn't imagine doing anything else. He thought again about another time and place when he thought he'd found his soul mate. He lost her too.

Spencer looked at the woman sitting across from him. She was adding cream and sweetener to her coffee and didn't catch on to the fact that he was staring. He didn't think Sadie would have a problem with sleeping with him. He ran his fingers through his hair because he couldn't believe he was having those thoughts about her. He'd been lonely and he thought she was too. He learned last year that she was widowed. Her husband had died a few years ago. He never saw her with anyone but noticed her gaze on him a time or two when she didn't think he'd been looking. He was very much aware of her. Maybe he should ask her to dinner sometime. It was a hell of a thing not to have a significant other in his life. He missed holding someone during the night but didn't feel like wading through the mine field of what women thought about his leg. Sadie never treated him like an invalid. She gave as good as she got. He'd been a real bastard to her and thought it was time to change that. He took a deep breath and asked, "You have any plans tonight?"

Sadie met his gaze with her own and couldn't believe it. Was he asking her out or just making small talk? She cleared her throat and replied, "I..." She shook her head and tried again, "No, I don't have any plans." He watched her tighten her hands around the coffee cup, "I usually go right home from work since I have a dog I need to walk when I get home." She sipped her coffee and looked down at the table, "Why do you ask?" Her eyes met his.

He shrugged, "I'm checking on a few more patients, then I'll be done for the evening over here and was going to head back across the bay." He took a deep breath and thought, "Here goes nothing." He cleared his throat and replied, "I didn't know if you'd like to have dinner with me?"

She couldn't stop the laughter that came out of her mouth, "What? Are you messing with me?" Sadie slammed her cup down and began to pull on her jacket, "You know, I thought for one minute that you could be decent and have a civil conversation and not be a jackass for once. I don't need this from you." She put her hand to her head, "I am so damn gullible. You think I'd learn."

She started to rise from the table when he placed his hand on top of hers. He took a breath and said, "Please don't leave. I promise you I wasn't being an ass. Please sit."

Sadie sat back down and waited for him to explain. He didn't keep her waiting for long, "Look, I know what a bastard I can be and I know I've been a real jerk to you in the past. I'm trying to be better when I'm around you, because you don't deserve how I've treated you." Spencer hesitated, "I don't want anyone pitying me and I tend to strike first. I don't know whether it's wrong or right, that's just what I do, okay?" He held her hand, "I'd like to take you to dinner to make it up to you. That's all." He looked away then his gaze met hers once more, "I'm lonely and thought you might be too. Just thought maybe us spending an evening together might be nice." When she continued to stare at him, he went for broke, "Look, Sadie, I like you, okay? I like how you don't put up with my bullshit and it'd be nice to share a meal with someone I don't have to try so damn hard with." Spencer shook his head, "Shit, that didn't come out like I meant it. What I meant was…" He stopped talking when she squeezed his hand.

"Spencer, I'd like to have dinner with you." She smiled and he watched her whole face light up, "Thank you for asking."

He let her hand go and said, "You're welcome." He sipped his coffee then asked, "Do you like Italian food? I know the owner of an Italian place. He's an old family friend and I'd like to take you to his restaurant. It's in Mobile so we wouldn't have to go far at all. I could pick you up at your house after I finish here. What do you say?"

Her eyes actually sparkled, "Yes," she said, "I'd like that very much." She fiddled with her napkin, and he noticed.

"Sadie?" he asked, "anything wrong?" He thought she looked nervous.

She glanced at him and sipped her coffee. She then cleared her throat, "You don't drink too much, do you?" She shifted in her seat, "I mean, I saw you pick up a glass of champagne at Hunt's wedding reception, but you only took a couple of sips and put it down. Then the rest of the time you had water. I just wanted to ask, um…"

177

He took a breath, "Sadie, just ask. What do you want to know?"

She replied, "When we go out tonight, do you mind if I order wine? I don't think you drink really and didn't know the reason. I didn't want to do anything to set you back if there's a problem with alcohol." She blew out a breath, "This is very awkward. Okay, are you a recovering alcoholic?"

He held his hand out and she placed her hand in his as he said, "Sadie, my father was the alcoholic, not me. I love my job too much to be an idiot about alcohol when seeing patients on a daily basis." She meshed her fingers with his and held on to his hand. He continued, "I detest the man. That's all I can say about it right now. Maybe another time, I'll tell you about why I hate my father as much as I do."

"Well, I did overhear you that night he came to your office. I'm sorry if I made you mad about listening to your conversation. I heard you talk about him cheating on your mother. You were very upset. I just wanted to help you. I want to apologize. I shouldn't have intruded that night. I'm sorry," she said. Sadie began to move her hand from his, but he held on. She looked up at him with wide eyes.

"Sadie, I want to clear up why I was so mad that night. It wasn't you. I'm the one who should apologize." He shook his head and said, "I haven't had that many people in my corner over the years. Of course, I have many colleagues I'm around every day. But, I've only had a few true friends like Hunt, my sister, and my mother. I'd like to make it up to you for how I've acted. It's just a fact of life that I don't invite too many into that inner circle. However, I'd like you to be one of those friends, if you don't mind."

"I'd like that," she answered, "I think I'll go check on Georgia now." She wrote her address on a napkin and gave it to him. He put it in his coat pocket. He followed her out of the cafeteria and she asked, "What time should I expect you tonight?"

He smiled, "Let's say 7:30. That too late for dinner?"

She smiled back, "No, not at all. I'm looking forward to it." She touched his arm, "Thanks Spencer. I'll see you soon."

He nodded and watched as she walked to the elevator and punched the button. He gazed at her as she waited. He liked her dark curly hair and the blue eyes that seem to see right through him. They suited her. He thought she was beautiful. When the door opened, she looked at him one more time and smiled. After the door closed, he took a deep breath and ran a hand down his face, "Oh, Mother of God, what have I done?" He put his hands in his pockets and thought about having dinner with Sadie tonight. Hopefully he wouldn't regret spending time with her. He hoped after tonight, that she wouldn't regret it either.

# Epilogue

*Six months later……*

Lillette woke up with the sun streaming through the bedroom window. She turned and collided with a well-muscled body. Her hands moved up his chest. She felt as if her heart stopped for a moment as she touched the scar where he'd been shot. She let out a breath and then touched his face. Her lips met his and he pulled her closer. She whispered, "Good morning husband. Are you awake?"

Strong arms roamed down her back, "Love, you're freezing." Calvin pulled her even closer, "You must have moved the air conditioner temp to the artic setting. You do realize it's October."

"Yes, October in Alabama. It was hot when I went to bed. I didn't realize how cold I'd gotten during the night." She inched closer to him, "Hmm, I'll just let you warm me up since my robe is on the floor along with your clothes."

He laughed, "Well, someone came into the kitchen last night looking so good after her bath with her robe on and her hair piled up on top of her head and gave me a look. I know what that look was all about."

She snuggled with him and pretended to be outraged, "I was just going to make me a cup of tea and then your eyes roamed down my body. What was I supposed to do when you walked over and unbelted my robe?"

He laughed and kissed her hand, "We almost didn't make it out of the kitchen."

She chuckled, "I wouldn't have minded."

"Really?" His eyes glittered, "Well, you just put a nice fantasy in my head." He ran his hands down her arms, "Let's see, the bistro table in there is not big enough. The floor would be too hard and cold." His eyes lit up and he rubbed his chin in thought, "You know, the walk-in pantry could be an option."

She grinned, "Calvin Wynfrey, I think I just created a monster." Her smile fled as his mouth moved to hers. He kissed her with a fervor that she never got tired of. They had married a month ago at a local 65-acre public garden located on what is known as Fowl River. Many friends, family members and colleagues watched the couple pledge their love to each other then joined them on the Great Lawn for a lovely reception. Even though it was still considered Alabama summer weather in September, the couple was fortunate that rain had come through the area a few hours before and cooled everything down. The breeze from the river helped. Large fans ran through the tent and cold drinks provided much relief from the heat. Guests were able to tour the gardens as well. It was a beautiful reception.

Lillette returned his kisses as she remembered their first night together as man and wife in this very bed. They had been a little nervous, but when they looked at each other, all their worry was soon forgotten. On their wedding night, they had touched each other with a desire only known to them, which soon turned to excitement to be together once more. It had been magical. Taking a few days of vacation time for their honeymoon had given them a chance to be alone. Never leaving their home in Washington Square, the happy couple loved one another, fed each other, then went right back to demonstrating their need to be together. New memories were made since their reconnection all those months ago. She spoke up, "So, my fine man, what would you like to do on this beautiful Saturday?"

"You think I'm fine?" He kissed her on the top of her head, then let his lips roam to her mouth.

She kissed him back then came up for air, "Hmm, you sure are." Her eyes crawled from his face, down to his six-pack abs, and lingered on his muscled thighs then back up again.

He laughed and hugged the woman he loved, "Oh, we are so going to enjoy our life." He gazed into her beautiful hazel eyes, "We could stay right here and I can show you how much I love you."

Lillette nodded her head, "That's true. But I already know how much you love me." Her eyes teased him, "You've shown me time after time after time. And very well if I may say so."

His eyes warmed with affection, "Well, my beautiful Lillette, I could take you out for a bike ride or a run." He smiled inside as he watched her roll her eyes, "Okay, we could go kayaking." Another eye roll flew in his direction, "How about we shower then go out for beignets and coffee, then call Georgia to see if we can stop by for a visit with our handsome little nephew?"

She swatted him on the arm and replied, "Now you're talking!" She then settled in his arms once more, "Although, I am pretty toasty and comfortable right this second in this wonderful bed with my husband." She moved in for a kiss and smoothed her arms down his shoulders, "Good Lord, you're incredible with these muscles of yours." She laughed when he flexed his shoulders and his arms. She kissed his chest then her gaze met his, "You know, now that I think about it, we could both use a little exercise this morning."

His eyes showed interest as he spoke up, "What'd you have in mind?

"Well, how about some push-ups?"

He looked into her eyes, "You want to see me show off, don't you? Do I have to get out of bed to do those?"

She shook her head, "Let me be more specific. We'd do those together, and we wouldn't have to get out of bed to do them." She raised an eyebrow and smiled like a cat with a bowl of cream.

"I like how you think." He rolled her way and asked, "Do you mind if I go first?" She caught her breath when he threw the covers off her and braced his arms on either side of her. He lowered himself over her, his lips meeting hers and he said, "That's one push up. You ready for the next one, Love?" Breathless with anticipation, she nodded her head and met his next kiss which sealed her love for him even more.

As the newlyweds perfected their morning workout, across town a doctor was waking up. Spencer Hawkins usually worked long hours delivering babies and seeing patients. His eyes landed on the clock next to his bed. He woke up a few hours earlier than the alarm, still bathed in sweat. It had been a particularly bad nightmare this time. The dream sequence had melded with reality. His father was bringing the boat around in the Gulf and this time the hit from the vessel just didn't take his leg. He floundered under the water, blood surrounding him. His body was pulled under. His sister didn't save him this time. He floated down. He couldn't pull himself to the surface. There was no one there to help him. He died.

A small hand reached over his shoulder and he flinched. He came back to the moment at hand. He turned slightly and there she was, Sadie Monroe. The doctor wasn't sure what to think about the lady next to him in his bed. They hadn't always gotten along when they were together at work. Spencer considered that more his fault. This was the first time he allowed anyone from his work life into his home and it had been a long time since he had anyone else in his bed. She wouldn't be here now, but he'd been tired and she wore him down since she found him in his office last night in pain and trying not to show it. He did exactly what this woman had accused him of many times. He had overdone it. Having a prosthetic leg never kept him from doing anything. But this time, she was right. The nurse practitioner he'd known for a while now drove him home, waited while he showered and then helped him into bed. She always showered at work and changed into street clothes to go home. He saw her leave their medical building many nights and had become accustomed to her routine.

He was too tired to protest when she laid down beside him, his prosthesis laying by the bed. Without any words being spoken, she realized he needed comfort from another human being. He thought about that and said to himself, "Sadie didn't blink an eye being in the same bed with a man who only had one leg." He worried about that with the opposite sex, but he didn't think anything threw this particular woman. He really admired her and liked her. He just didn't know how to show her or tell her how he felt, but he thought he was getting a little better about that. They'd gone out a few times for dinner after work and a couple of times for lunch on the weekends. It had been nice being with her. Spencer even stayed around a couple of times and took a walk with her and her dog. Being an animal lover, he hadn't minded.

Spencer realized he wanted more from Sadie, but he was a selfish ass when it came to showing his feelings. Maybe he was more like his old man than he thought. Now there was a true bastard. He shook his head and came back to the present. The doctor felt a gentle hand move from his shoulder across to his midsection. She snuggled into his back and he liked the feel of her nestled into his body. He wouldn't mind turning over all the way and pulling her into him and distancing himself from thinking about his pain or his life without his leg. He just couldn't do it to her. She had become important to him and she didn't need a grumpy asshole to deal with on a personal level. He had too much baggage and she was too good for him. But that didn't stop him from moving his hand to clasp hers to his stomach and hold it there. He heard her breathing smooth out and realized she was asleep. A calm awareness reached him and he regulated his breathing. He tightened his hand on hers and let sleep claim him. When he dreamed again, she was there, saving his life.

*Thank you for reading Love's Redemption. The 7th book in the Over the Bay Series will be coming next! Thank you to the readers for your support!*

Deborah McDonald

*Book 7 in the Over the Bay Series coming soon!*

Authors previous books:

Available on Amazon

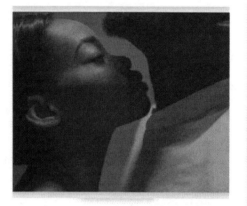

# Acknowledgements

Thanks as always to my family and friends for being so supportive of my creative endeavors. I appreciate all of the feedback and enjoyment of the series.

Thank you to the Facebook friends who gave me great ideas and answer many questions to take my writing into another direction or sometimes another hemisphere! :)

To Noah "Trey" Oliver—kudos to you for all the information about law enforcement, what kind of handcuffs are out there now (I just know what I see on TV shows!) and the hierarchy of the law in Mobile, AL.

Jaime Betbeze---I feel like you are the expert in all things Mobile! Thank you for the information about what is allowed on homes in Washington Square and in the OGD! (especially historic homes)

I appreciate all those business owners in Old Towne Daphne. You inspire me every day.

To the Pensters—thanks for all of the support and illumination of what being a writer means.

GOOGLE is my guide to answering questions about cars and history.

Deborah Navarro—as always, thank you for your love of editing.

John O'Melveny Woods—my publisher... Thanks for your advice and guidance.

I would like to thank my cousins, Lisa, Mary Kaye, and Karen, for allowing me to include their mother, Rowena in this book. Visiting my relatives in New Orleans for years led us to have some interesting times with the family. I had another great aunt, named Genevieve, who was close to Aunt Rowena. Sadly, both ladies have passed on, but their memories will always be a part of our lives. I have brought them back to life, if only for a little while. They weren't sisters, but I thought that would add to the story if I made them that way. If you knew both these ladies, you would know that they had strength and a style all their own.

Aunt Genevieve was actually an Auxiliary Lady for Providence Hospital in Mobile. Aunt Rowena was a member of the Krewe of Orpheus, which was started by Harry Connick, Jr in New Orleans. In the book, I took the liberty of making a story twist in which Harry rides on the float with Aunt Rowena. Many afternoons, our mother would take us to visit Aunt Genevieve so she could have coffee with her. As southern ladies do, coffee was poured into a fine china cup with a saucer. A silver spoon (that I am sure she polished) would be on the table. Aunt

Rowena was a nurse and sold real estate later in life. She loved antiques. May they rest in peace.

From left to right: Rowena Christensen, Genevieve Smith and Mary Alice Rice

Deborah McDonald is a local author who lives in Daphne, Alabama. Her first published book, Jubilee Sunset Romance, is the beginning of the Over the Bay Series.

Deborah wrote her first essay in college, which was included in a university English textbook. It was a highlight of her college career. A wife and mother, Deborah has worked as an educator for over 32 years.

**https://deborahmcdonaldauthor.com/**

Additional books by the author

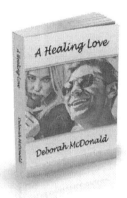

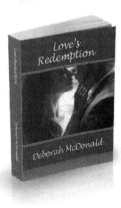
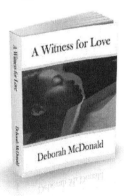

Made in the USA
Columbia, SC
10 March 2023

13481964R00117